PAPER
SOLDIERS

A DCI PRIEST NOVEL

PAPER SOLDIERS

MARK PETTINGER

ISBN: 979-8-5616-7215-6

ALSO BY MARK PETTINGER
The Decalogue
Tick Tock Time's Up

CHAPTER 1

D eefer......Deefer......where the bloody hell are you?'
Just as she had finished calling for the second time, he
finally came into sight, bounding through the thick
carpet of colourful bluebells and bursts of wood anemones
and celandines, his ears flopping around and his tongue
hanging from his mouth, panting like he had sprinted
along every woodland trail already.

'There you are; you shouldn't go running off where
Mummy can't see you.' The dog was clearly none the wiser
after his brief verbal berating, he just wanted to run off
and explore.

These were *his woods,* where he had walked, run and
generally lost himself for years. Whether the ground was
covered in bright and colourful flowers, or a thick layer of
fresh snow that would stick to his fur like cotton, he would
rampage his way through, exploring every inch with the
same boundless energy and enthusiasm.

Mrs Sproston had been walking in Oakwood Lane
Woods for just over twenty minutes with her King Charles
spaniel. He had been named 'Deefer' by her eldest son a
number of years ago after she had *allowed* him to name
their new puppy. It was an exciting time in the household,

1

and the whole family were swept up in the intoxicating buoyancy that the little bundle of fur would bring to daily family life, so she promised her son that he was in charge of naming the new addition to the family. It was to become a decision that she would live to regret many times since, and although she could have asserted her parental authority and overruled her son at the time, she chose to accept his naming of their puppy.

'D…Dee…what? Deeeff. Sorry, Paul, I don't get it. What do you want to call him?'

'Deefer, Mum, I want to call him Deefer.'

'Deefer?'

'Yes, Deefer,' said her son, clearly believing that a further breakdown of the proposed name would be necessary, 'D-E-E-F-E-R.'

'What kind of name is that for a dog?'

'Deefer; Deefer dog.'

'What? You've lost me, Paul.'

'Deefer dog; you know…d for dog.'

'You have got to be kidding me,' she said with some exasperation, 'you want to call your dog, our dog, Deefer dog?'

'Yes.'

'Why?'

'Because it's funny, and it's original.'

'It's not original, Paul, it's bloody stupid; and there's no way in hell that I am taking a dog for a walk, in a public place, shouting bloody Deefer.'

It took many months, but, Emily Sproston had eventually got used to the unusual name for the family dog, and had even got used to calling out his name when Deefer had run off, which of course he regularly did as soon as he was let off the lead. As long as she didn't have to shout loudly, and in the presence of others; although there had been one or two times, over the past two years, where Deefer had been noticeable by his absence, and Emily had needed to shout, and quite loudly, in order to call him back. On each occasion she had felt quite self-conscious around the hundred or so people that were present within her immediate vicinity in the busy open parkland. In those situations, it would clearly have been preferable to have a dog called 'Charlie', or alternatively and preferably, a husband or son present that would have shouted 'Deefer'. Nevertheless, she loved Deefer as one of the family. *Stupid bloody name.*

Emily Sproston had been walking deep into the woods for about twenty minutes. The woods themselves were vast, and covered almost forty-five acres, but there were half a dozen or so well-trodden walking routes, of which she knew every inch of every one. The different routes through the woods provided opportunities and options for a quick fifteen-minute amble, covering about a mile, through to a twelve-mile hike that might occupy most walkers for three hours or so. She enjoyed walking the dog for hours on end, and had in earlier years walked these woods extensively with her husband and son too; mainly on warm summer or breezy autumnal Sunday afternoons, before retiring to a local pub for a spot of Sunday lunch, and the best part of a bottle of Pinot Grigio. Those days had unfortunately long gone as her son, Paul, now wanted to spend his Sundays with his girlfriend, and her husband's arthritis in his knees meant that a walk before lunch was out of the question. The family walks might have gone, but thankfully the Sunday lunches had remained on most weekends.

Catching the time at eight twenty-five, she knew that the next right-hand bend opened up a fork in the path, the left side of which would mark her halfway point, and pave the way for the return to where she had parked the car. As she approached the bend in the path, she looked around to ensure that Deefer was with her, or at least within vision. He wasn't, but then that wasn't anything new. She frequently retold the same story to her husband of how she had 'enjoyed' separate walks to Deefer; how she had let him out of car, and then perhaps caught sight of him once or twice during her usual sixty-minute walk; then finally smiled broadly and with more than a degree of relief when he was always already sitting waiting by the car, after she reached the end of the trail. He wasn't within sight, but he could be heard. She could hear Deefer barking, and her ears told her that he was not too far ahead of her. As she rounded the corner towards the fork in the road, she saw him. He was sitting in the middle of the trail, looking up at a large mature oak tree, a tree that that had grown majestically over the past fifty years, into the one-hundred-foot beast it was today. A tree that was well known and loved by walkers within the woods, and one that marked the fork in the trail and a division of alternate paths.

It took Emily less than a second to identify with the reason for her dog's apparent vocal overload. What surprised her was how calmly she reacted thereafter. She walked over to Deefer, and proceeded to rub his neck and pat him on the back.

'Shh, shh, Deefer, shh.' Almost immediately the dog stopped barking, but did not avert his eyes from the tree. Panting heavily, he looked up at her, expecting her to do something.

Emily reached into her coat pocket and retrieving her mobile phone, she hit the single button of the only number that she needed in this situation – 999.

CHAPTER 2

D CI Priest sat in his car for a moment, looking out of the windscreen towards the sky. It was daylight for sure, but the sun was never going to break through those dark stormy clouds.

He hoped that he would be finished here before the rain came, but as he pulled on his heavy waterproof coat, and swapped his comfortable leather shoes for his green wellies, he was going to ensure that he stayed dry, whatever was to come. He checked his watch... nine-forty a.m.

Priest was met at the start of the woodland trail by a uniformed officer, who had been stationed there by his sergeant, specifically to guide the numerous expected attendees and to ensure that they didn't take the wrong trail, wandering around aimlessly looking for and hoping to stumble across the crime scene. Although having only been at the scene for fifteen minutes himself, guiding people down the correct route was a big ask of the young officer. The walk was fairly brisk, and they reached the fork in the trail much quicker than the usual Sunday morning rambler would. Not that there were to be any more ramblers or further dog walkers this Sunday morning. The woods could be accessed via three main entry points, and unformed officers had been positioned at each, apparently already busy turning away those that had arrived for their weekly dose of fresh air and exercise. *Sorry, the woods are closed today* was all that the officers would, or could, say to those they had watched pull up into the car park and spend ten minutes dressing appropriately for the elements before walking over to the start of their nearest trail. It was to be almost two hours before anyone used their initiative and closed the entrances to the car parks.

As Priest rounded the corner, his eyes expected to meet with what he would call a 'usual' crime scene: the immediate area around the body would generally be cordoned off with a large white tent to protect the scene from further forensic contamination, or at worst, total loss of any forensic evidence should the impending torrential rain wash it all away. However, there was no obligatory pitched tent this morning; the area, the body, was covered by a large screen that extended some ten feet in height, and had been erected using metal poles, made sturdy with heavy bases, and tarpaulin hooked and wrapped around the poles. There was a uniformed officer standing next to the tarpaulin screen, and numerous SOCO officers, some huddled in a group talking, others nipping in and out of a gap in the tarpaulin. He caught the eye of two of his detectives; DS Stephens and DC Simkins.

'Bloody hell, are you sure that you are wrapped up enough?' asked a cheeky Stephens. Simkins joined in with the brief chuckle at their boss's expense.

'All you're missing is one of those oversized, rubber-looking fisherman's hats with the large brim,' she added.

'You won't be laughing in an hour or so when the heavens open and it starts to bucket down. Have you seen those clouds?' He comically pointed to the sky, like the detectives needed help in understanding where to find the clouds. 'This whole place will become a bloody quagmire, and you will be wishing that you were wearing wellies and a thick waterproof coat.'

Simkins tugged at his own lightweight navy jacket. 'I'll be fine, guv, and don't you worry about me.' His jacket was so lightweight it could have easily have been one of those kagools that can be folded away in a handy sized bag; the ones that your mum bought for you and made you take with you on your school trip to Twycross Zoo, even though the weather presenter on the morning television breakfast show was predicting twenty degrees and sun all day. It was the kind of jacket that 'went missing' on school trips, never to be seen again; *dunno, Mum, I probably left it at the zoo, sorry.*

'Funnily enough, Robert, I don't tend to waste time worrying about you,' he smiled at them both and tugged at his own coat, then turned his attention back to the situation, 'so, I only received a very short brief over the phone, but tell me what we have.'

'Good morning, detective chief inspector.' DS Stephens hadn't managed to commence her update for Priest before the police doctor came rushing in, and crashed their threesome. 'What do you have for me, on this bright spring morning?'

Priest looked up towards the grey clouds and the rapidly darkening gloomy sky, before returning his gaze to the doctor. 'I have no idea, doctor, I have only just arrived myself. Why don't you go with my detective and find out, and I'll join you shortly.' He motioned to DC Simkins to escort the doctor towards the body.

'Sorry, Nic, you were saying?'

'Sure; we have a woman out walking her dog this morning, she found the body about twenty minutes into her walk. She called 999; the call was logged at eight forty-two this morning. The first uniform arrived on the scene at eight fifty-five, and Robert and I arrived a few minutes later. The body was found by Mrs Sproston.' DS Stephens pointed towards where she was standing with a uniformed officer. 'I'll introduce you in a minute.'

'That's fine, Nic, thanks. Let's have a look at the body first shall we?'

'Sure. I have to say, Jonny, I haven't seen anything quite like this before.'

'Really…Why?'

'You'll see.'

'Okay, let's have a look.'

They walked over to the area underneath the large oak tree, and the officer held open a gap in the tarpaulin screen, through which Priest and Stephens stepped. There were three people to be found within the cordoned off area; the two SOCO officers were standing to the side, temporarily keeping out of the way of the police doctor as he was making a preliminary assessment of the body.

But it wasn't the three erect, moving, and very much alive people that caught the attention of Priest. His gaze fixed squarely on the mature oak tree, which had to be a good two metres in diameter, but on which was…and there was no better way of describing it in his mind…a man, crucified.

The man was black, of Caribbean origin, although Priest's knee-jerk assessment of his nationality or parental heritage, was borne solely from the sweeping generalisation of seeing his impressive set of dreadlocks and mature, yet neat, beard. He had been stripped naked, and a quick scan of the ground showed there appeared to be no clothes visible in the immediate area, although they might have been inspected and cleared by the SOCO team already. His arms were bound together with rope, one hand pressed firmly against the other with a large iron nail protruding from his wrist. The resultant blood loss had seeped from his wrist and created a trail that snaked its way down his arm and his torso, dripping onto his slightly outstretched right knee before running down his shin and foot, and finally creating a small pool on the woodland floor. The blood loss had ceased some time ago, and the wound on the wrists had clearly started to congeal, turning from a bright red into a dark crimson oak red.

His legs had been bound in rope too. Multiple lengths of the thick double braided rope around his thighs, and more around his ankles. One ankle had been placed in front of the other, and a large iron nail had been driven, with the massive force it would have needed, through both feet.

His body didn't appear to exhibit any further signs of trauma, not that being crucified was a lightweight way to die by any stretch of the imagination, but there were no other wounds immediately visible – knife or bullet; his face didn't appear to have been comparable to ten rounds in the ring with Mike Tyson. As best as they could see at this point with his dark skin, there were no bruises or other lacerations.

'Well,' said the doctor as he turned from the body to face the detectives, 'shall I tell you the bleeding obvious, or do you think that you probably have that covered already?'

11

'Let's go through the motions please, doctor,' affirmed Priest.

'Okay. Well, from my initial assessment, I would say that he has been dead for between eight to twelve hours, and whilst I cannot be certain at this stage, it appears that death was due to suffocation.'

Despite not being medically qualified in the slightest, Priest felt the need to challenge the doctor in his statement. 'Suffocation? Are you sure that death wasn't caused by exsanguination, doctor?'

The doctor was about to respond and explain that, in his opinion, the detective had misunderstood the medical terminology, either that or he was overtly surprised that Priest knew any words with five syllables. But Priest jumped in. 'Yes, massive blood loss, and thank you, doctor. I do listen and learn sometimes to the medical terminology.'

They all shared a smile.

'Surely the nail, however large it is, and with whatever force it was driven through both his hands and feet, wouldn't be sufficient to bleed him dry?' asked Stephens.

'Very observant, sergeant. Top marks.'

'Teacher's pet,' Priest murmured under his breath. She smiled back at him.

'The crucifixion would, and did, result in significant blood loss, but the act itself would not have led to his death, even after several days.'

'Go on…' Priest prompted the doctor to elaborate further.

'Exsanguination, or significant blood loss causing death as you correctly defined, chief inspector, has very rarely been the actual cause of death following someone's crucifixion. It is the injuries and exposure that generally determine the cause of death; either the body loses so much oxygen that the person smothers, or the carbon dioxide in the body increases to the extent that the body tissues turn acidic and destroy their own cells.'

'That doesn't sound like a quick process.'

'It sounds like bloody torture to me,' Stephens added.

'In the main, no, you are correct. However the former explanation, suffocation, can occur and lead to death in hours, rather than days.'

'Do you have any thoughts as to why he has been nailed through his wrists, and not his palms, doctor?'

'I do actually, yes. Despite the hundreds of images throughout history depicting it to be so, very few people were actually crucified with nails through their hands. If you think about it, putting a person's whole weight on a relatively delicate piece of flesh would simply tear the hand enough that the person could pull the nail back through their hand, and free their upper body. People were crucified through the wrists, as this was much harder to tear yourself loose. Sadistic, yes, but yet a totally pragmatic solution.'

Priest had been interested up to this point, but was starting to drift off as it looked like the doctor was only part way through his monologue.

'What is interesting with this crucifixion, detectives, although I doubt it is intentional, is that he was crucified with his arms over his head.'

'Okay, what's the relevance, or importance or that?' asked Stephens.

'Well, he could have been positioned in a more tradi-tional way, a position that supports the thought that a cross is required for a crucifixion. It isn't, although the girth of this huge oak tree would certainly allow for his arms to be spread and pinned horizontally. When people are crucified with their arms stretched out above their head, this makes it very difficult to breathe. Once the muscles give out, it is excruciating as the shoulders separate from the sockets and the overall arm can lengthen by inches. From there the chest would sag downwards. It's easy to inhale with arms fully outstretched, but difficult to exhale again. The body needs to work its muscles to breathe in and out, and it is used to doing so with little resistance. Once the chest is fully expanded, it's impossible to breathe in anything more than sips of air. The victim slowly suffocates, unable to get enough oxygen, over the course of several hours.'

'Aside from the obvious medical relevance, how do you know so much about crucifixion, doctor?' Stephens asked. Priest gave her a reproving glance, knowing only too well that she had yet again opened the door to a potential further ten minutes of verbal diarrhoea from the incomparable, if not omnipotent, blessed doctor.

'Well, many years ago as part of my pathology PhD, I wrote a paper on the causal effects of crucifixion on the human body. So what I don't know on the subject isn't worth knowing.'

'Apparently so,' noted Priest.

'How amazing,' replied Stephens, 'time to rekindle that grey matter in the investigation of this victim.'

'Indeed, sergeant. One final observation if I may, chief inspector.' Priest nodded, 'Look at how his feet have been nailed to the tree, and specifically how his legs and feet have been positioned. Again, I'm not sure if this was intentional, and done with any degree of knowledge, skill or indeed any experience, but nailing someone's feet and how the lower body is treated, could have an effect on how long the person lived.'

'Okay....' *In for a penny, in for a pound,* Priest thought. 'How so?'

The doctor moved closer to the body and pointed towards the lower limbs. 'You can see that his feet have been nailed to the tree, obviously. I would argue that his knees have been placed at a forty-five degree angle. A person's natural reaction would be to try and support themselves by putting pressure on their injured feet, but it would only be a matter of time before their legs gave away as well, due mainly to the fact that their legs were bent.'

'What would the pain have been like, doctor? What would he have felt? Would he have been alive?' DS Stephens started to pepper questions at the doctor as quickly as they popped into her mind.

'I can confirm that he was alive when he was initially crucified; and not that it helps in any way with your investigation, but I can confirm that his last few hours before he passed out would have been lived in excruciating pain; struggling for every breath as his life ebbed away in slow motion.'

'Thank you, doctor,' answered Priest and Stephens almost simultaneously.

'My pleasure.' And with that, he turned his back to the detectives and returned to the dead, naked body that was nailed to the oak tree.

Priest and Stephens exited the makeshift screen, and made their way towards the lady who had found the body.

'Guv, this is Mrs Emily Sproston.' Stephens made the introduction and Priest stepped forward.

Emily Sproston looked considerably fresher than her actual forty-three years. Standing about five foot nine inches, she had light-ash blonde hair that had been tied back in a ponytail. She was what Priest would call part of the 'horsey brigade'; due mainly to her appearance: Hunter wellies, Joules polo shirt and matching quilted jacket, and no doubt a middle-class accent. Priest had no idea if she owned a horse or not, he didn't care. Perhaps she owned a stable and the twenty horses that came with it….God, he hated bloody horses, and the snooty 'horsey brigade'.

'Mrs Sproston, hello, I'm Detective Chief Inspector Priest.'

Mrs Sproston held out her hand, but noted that the detective's had not been offered, so she quickly withdrew it into her jacket pocket, feeling both slightly embarrassed and mildly offended.

'So, my officers tell me that you arrived this morning around eight o'clock; parked your car, then started through the woods with your dog.'

'That's right, yes.'

'It was about twenty past eight, was it, when you came around the corner and saw the body?' The question was asked rhetorically, but his brief pause at the end allowed Emily Sproston to offer her affirmation once again.

'Did you see anyone else during your twenty-minute walk this morning?'

'No; actually it was unusually quiet. I might normally see one or two regulars at that time, but Deefer and I had the woods to ourselves it seemed.'

Priest was about to pick up on the 'Deefer' reference, but a slight touch on the arm from Stephens told him that he should leave it alone.

'Did you touch or move anything, Mrs Sproston, you know, perhaps out of curiosity?'

'Curiosity, chief inspector, no I bloody did not. I think that I have remained rooted to this same spot since I came around that corner.'

'Of course, silly question. Anyway, thank you for your time and I'm sorry that you had to witness this. If you would kindly wait here for another ten or fifteen minutes, one of my officers will take a brief statement and confirm your contact details, then you can be on your way.'

'That's fine, thank you, officer.'

Officer, officer! Priest resisted the temptation to correct her, despite the fact that she had got his rank correctly the first time. He was an 'officer' after all, just *a bloody senior one.*

'We might need to call on you again over the next few days. If we need to speak to you again, we will try and call ahead.' He didn't wait for a response, and turned away.

Thirty minutes passed, during which time Priest had ascertained that there were no clothes to be found anywhere near the body. Priest had ordered, and unusually joined in, a one-hundred-metre radius search of the area, looking for any discarded clothes. The numbers of officers at the scene was probably a little too light to undertake this type of radial search, but Priest instructed it to be done anyway. They came up empty-handed.

As he was walking back towards the body, a young uniformed officer stepped into his path, and enquired, 'it is Powell, isn't it, sir?'

'Sorry...Powell?'

'Yes, guv, I think I recognise the body.'

The period of silence thereafter spurred Priest to prompt the young constable, 'and?'

'I think it is a guy called Jarel Powell.'

'Jarel Powell. His name rings a bell, but I can't place it. Why should I know it, officer…?'

'Hudson, sir, PC Hudson.'

'Sorry, yes.' For the life of him, Priest couldn't think why he was apologising for not knowing the officer's name.

'Jarel Powell is part of the Yardie gang that controls a lot of the drugs in and around Manchester, guv.'

'So, how come you recognise him, constable?'

'He has quite a reputation, you might say he is infamous around Manchester. I haven't come across him personally, I guess you might be better off speaking to the drug squad, sir.'

'Thanks, I will.' Priest wandered off, back towards his colleagues.

'I think I might know who our victim is, Nic,' said Priest with an air of confident nonchalance.

'Really?'

'Yes, really.'

'Go on then, amaze me.'

'His name is Jarel Powell, and he is one of the top dogs within one of the Yardie drug gangs from Manchester.'

'Okay,' said Stephens, a little surprised that Priest would know such a person existed, 'and you know this how?'

'I'm a walking, talking encyclopaedia of Manchester's criminal underworld, me, Nic,' he said once again with a hint of nonchalant sarcasm. He paused for effect.

'No, I'm only joking. I've just been chatting to the constable over there; he told me that he believes our victim is Powell. Apparently, he is quite infamous around some of the more salubrious of Manchester's inner city shit-holes.'

Stephens smiled. 'I wasn't aware that you were too familiar with the highlights of Manchester's less affluent areas, either.'

'Just a guess, Nic, just a guess. Anyway, can you have Stacey run a complete background check on him, ready to give us a rundown when we get back to the station? It might not be him, but ask Stacey to do the work, and we might get an early lead, and confirmation, on the ID.'

'Sure, will do,' she confirmed.

'Anything else?'

'The forensic boys have been asking about the various footprints around the tree and on the trails leading in and away, and if they should take photos or moulds.'

'I don't think that we need to bother with any three-dimensional casts, nor any footprints along the trails. This place is clearly very popular with walkers, and I dare say that there have been hundreds of different boots through here in the last few days, most of which are still impressed within the soil. Ask the SOCO boys to take some high quality photos of the imprints around the circumference of the tree, categorise them back at the lab, and fire them across to the incident room as digital images. I don't think that it will help us at this stage, but you never know, it might prove to be useful when we have a suspect, and a pair of size tens in our hands that we are looking to match.'

'What about the tyre tracks? Same question from the boys.'

'Tyre tracks…What tyre tracks?'

'Apparently, and I haven't seen it myself, if you walk down the trail to the right-hand side of the tree for about one hundred metres, you reach a perpendicular track which is wide enough for vehicular access. So arguably our suspect could have driven the body some way into the woods before ending up here. The doctor has told us that our victim was still alive when he was brought here, but might not have been conscious, and our suspect might have used the track to get closer into the woods.'

'Are there tyre tracks, or is that a silly question?'

'There are half a dozen, I'm told.'

'Okay, ask the boys to take some photos, and to try and match the treads with specific tyre manufacturers. Tell them not to bust their balls on it though; again it might only help us down the line when we have a suspect, and a potential vehicle, but it's not going to be of immediate use to us. Thanks, Nic.'

'Okay, will do.'

'Right, I'm off back to the station. I've got to see Superintendent Sawden in about an hour.'

'Are you in trouble with the boss again, Jonny?'

'No, little miss smarty-pants, I'm not. I have to attend a quarterly budgetary and resource meeting.'

'Yaaawwwwnnnnnn,' Stephens replied, matching the audible response with a visual one.

'I'll see you back at the station, Nic.'

Just as Priest was walking away down the trail, she called out to him, 'hang on a minute,' and Priest stopped and turned around. 'Today is Sunday.'

'Yes, very observant; we'll make a detective of you yet, Nic.'

'No, I mean, you're attending a quarterly budgetary meeting, with Sawden, on a Sunday?'

'Yep, sure am. Margaret has been trying to align diaries for three weeks on this. Three times the meeting has been set, only for me to cancel at the last minute when something came up. Sawden knew I was the senior officer on duty this weekend, so he offered to come in on Sunday.'

'Ah, okay. It's a good job that you haven't cancelled again then, you know, what with having a dead drug dealer crucified against a tree in the middle of the woods.'

Priest smiled, 'I can't cancel again, Nic, not even with this happening this morning.'

CHAPTER 3

Have we heard back from the doctor yet?' asked Priest, pushing through the double doors and striding into the incident room.

'Yes, guv, we have actually,' replied DC Wright, standing up from her chair, 'Doctor Bell has just corroborated the identification of our victim. The dental records also match the fingerprints that were taken.'

Priest punctuated an unnecessary and uneasy pause in the conversation; '….and, Stacey?'

'Oh yes, sorry, guv. Our victim is indeed Jarel Lamar Powell.'

'Great. Do we have an address?'

'Yes, guv.'

'Good. Has DS Stephens returned from the crime scene yet?'

'No, guv, they haven't arrived back yet.'

'Okay, grab your coat, Stacey, then meet me in the car park in ten minutes.'

'Where are we going, guv?'

'We, Stacey, have the unenviable shit job of telling Mrs Powell that her good-for-nothing, drug dealing, scumbag of a husband was discovered in a local wood strung up by his bollocks; and that the world, probably if not most definitely, is a much better place because of it.'

Unusually for Stacey Wright, she had cottoned on to the sarcasm and was quick with her own retort. 'I think that you had better leave the talking up to me this time, guv.'

Priest smiled back at her.

The three miles to the Powell family home in Moss Side took almost twenty-five minutes, and with Priest cursing at every traffic light and moronic driver that delayed him, the journey was less than enjoyable. But it was the weight of the overall traffic that mainly contributed to the longer than expected journey, and Priest was adamant that even in his relatively short time in Manchester, the volume of vehicles on the road appeared to have doubled.

Stacey chose not to offer any sort of opinion, and simply let him continue muttering his expletive-filled diatribe on all things congestion and traffic related.

'And what's more....' Stacey switched off, and he eventually ran out of steam.

Jarel Powell and his family lived in a four-bedroom detached house in The Maine Place, a cul-de-sac just off Maine Road. The development was quite new, having been built on the former Manchester City FC ground. The old stadium had been demolished in 2004, and the subsequent few years had seen a development of almost four hundred modern houses built. All of them had been sold, many of them initially off-plan; but over half of the houses had since been resold by investors cashing in and making a few quid in the buoyant property market over the subsequent decade.

As Priest and DC Wright pulled off Maine Road and into the cul-de-sac, they saw, well, exactly what they expected to see – a selection of modern detached, semi-detached and town houses. It was what it was – suburbia. Perhaps not the type of house that a big-time drug dealer might usually choose as their home. From their past experience and knowledge, the homes of drug dealers could generally be found at opposite ends of the spectrum; either multi-million-pound mansions in gated communities, ostentatious and overly flamboyant, their owners clearly flaunting, and spending, some of their illegally achieved wealth. The other end of the spectrum saw drug dealers, potentially just as wealthy, choose to remain and live in the inner city areas in which they grew up, and which provided both their customers' and their income. They chose to remain in a house, in an area, where they felt more safe and secure. Powell's house was neither one nor the other; he chose to hide in plain sight; in suburban Manchester.

Priest pulled up outside of the house and switched off the engine.

'Stacey, I'm sure that you brought yourself up to speed before we left, but just as a recap; his wife is called Delanna, and I understand they have two boys, Aston and Jontry. Obviously I'm not sure if the young boys are going to be there, but just as important, I'm not sure if any of his gang members are going to be there. I don't expect any trouble, which is why it's just you and me.'

'Okay.' DC Wright hadn't been feeling the least bit anxious, until this point.

'If for any bizarre reason it starts to kick off, which granted would be exceptional considering the reason we are here, let's just retreat to the car.'

'Okay, guv, understood.' Her nerves hadn't been calmed by their brief exchange of dialogue, but she drew a deep breath and readied herself. *It's a good job that I've got my Wonder Woman knickers on,* she thought to herself. She then thought about sharing that with Priest, to add a little brevity, but quickly retracted any such thoughts or actions.

As he exited the car, Priest stood for a second and viewed the house. It was as modern detached house with a stylish curved garden wall; the small front lawn appeared neatly cropped, and borders underneath the front window were planted with several dwarf conifers. *Definitely not the house of a bloody Yardie drug lord,* he thought to himself.

A quick rattle on the white uPVC door with the knuckles, and a few seconds later it opened.

'Good afternoon.' Priest took out his warrant card and held it aloft, shortly followed by Stacey Wright, 'are you Delanna Powell?'

'Mi don't talk te no babylon.' The would-be gangster's moll had clearly taken a leaf from her husband's book on the expected, if not accepted, way to speak to the police.

'Mrs Powell, my name is Detective Chief Inspector Priest, and this is Detective Constable Wright.'

'Mi tink yah come layta wen Jarel at ome.' She started to close the door as Priest stepped forward and wedged his hand in between the door and its frame, much to his discomfort as the door closure trapped his hand.

'Jarel is the reason that we have come to talk to you, Mrs Powell.' He purposely left a brief pause, as his follow-up was going to sting a little. 'Oh, and drop the Jamaican patois; I know you're a local girl that was born and raised in Manchester.'

She opened the door a little more and Priest released his hand. 'We need to speak to you, Mrs Powell, it's important, can we come in please?'

Delanna Powell defiantly tutted her acceptance of his request, then turned and walked back into the house, leaving the door open for them to enter.

Priest and DC Wright were reluctantly led into the first room immediately off the hallway, the lounge. The lounge, or at least the interior design and decoration of it, was not he had expected; it was normal; in fact, just like any, if not all other lounges across the country. The interior was just like the outside of the house, normal. Jarel Powell and his family lived in normal, suburban Manchester. Priest was unsure what to expect: ornamental samurai swords mounted on the wall, the odd 9mm Beretta scattered around with a couple of bricks of cocaine were, in hindsight, not likely to be adorning the lounge, even that of one of Manchester's premier drug lords.

'Take a seat, please, Mrs Powell.' Priest gestured with his hand towards the large black leather sofa behind where she was standing. The detectives took a seat too on the facing sofa.

'Mrs Powell, I'm afraid that we come with some bad news. There's no easy way to break this; I'm sorry to tell you that your husband, Jarel, has died.'

'Sorry,' came Delanna's instant and expected reflex response, as she looked for the detective to repeat what she must have misheard the first time around.

'I'm sorry, Mrs Powell, your husband was found dead earlier this morning.'

'No, no, no, no, no, no, this is not right; Jarel is not dead.'

'I'm sorry. I know this must be a terrible shock for you. Is there someone that we can call for you?' DC Wright asked.

They sat in silence for what seemed an eternity to the detectives, but in reality was little more than ten seconds; but the dead air appeared simply to serve as an opportunity for Delanna Powell to compose herself.

'How did he die?'

'Well, he was found earlier this morning in Oakwood Lane Woods by a woman walking her dog. I can't really say too much at the minute in relation to how he died, but it does look like he was murdered.'

'Murdered. Who would want to murder Jarel? He was a loving man, a kind man, a family man.'

'From what I hear, Mrs Powell, your husband might have had quite a few enemies.' DCI Priest took the opportunity to brush past the softly-softly approach and steam ahead with questions directly linking the known gang affiliations. 'I assume that he came into contact with a whole host of people over the past few years that he angered in some way, or that may have wanted to take over from him.'

'Take over from him, what do you mean?'

'Yes, it's as likely that the perpetrator of his murder was known to Jarel, just as much as it might be a stranger or enemy, Mrs Powell.'

'My Jarel didn't have any enemies, he was a businessman.'

'Mrs Powell, we are trying to be sympathetic due to the obvious sensitive nature of the news that we have just conveyed; but your husband, as I'm sure you well know, was the head of one of the most notorious and successful drug gangs in the north west of England.'

'I don't know anything about drugs and gangs.'

Priest chose not to continue to press the point, and the detectives left after a further ten minutes. The initial shock was clearing and realisation was dawning on Delanna

Powell that her husband, scumbag of a drug dealer that he was, was dead. The detectives promised to keep her updated with information, and advised that they would probably need to return the next day to talk to her again. After a further and final request to call a friend or neighbour was rejected, the detectives left Delanna Powell alone and in tears.

CHAPTER 4

'Just pull up here.'

'Why?'

'Because we're early.'

The driver checked his watch. 'No we're not, we're bang on time.'

'Just pull up here because I fucking said so then.'

The driver of the Ford Transit van indicated to pull over to the kerbside, but didn't switch off the engine. As the vehicle came to a halt, he unfastened his seatbelt and laid his head back on the headrest. Ritual use of the indicators and the wearing of a seatbelt wasn't generally associated with the 'white van man' on British roads; but this van driver was shortly to be taking control of over a million pounds street value of Class A drugs, and getting pulled for a minor traffic violation was to be avoided at all costs.

'What are we waiting for, Davey? Can we not just crack on and get them on board?' No reply received. 'Davey…'

'Shut the fuck up, I'm concentrating.'

'On…'

'Let me do the thinking, and talking, and planning, and organising,' his voice was projecting louder and louder with each word, 'and you just drive the fucking van. Alright?'

'Yes, Davey.'

'Good.' After a brief pause, he said, 'right, let's go. Slowly.'

The Ford Transit van pulled up to the large steel gates, standing eight foot high, and being the secondary vehicular entrance to Liverpool Docks. The main entrance, used by ninety-nine percent of vehicles, was to be found on the other side of the docks. This seldom used entrance was always kept locked and permanently manned by a security guard.

As the van pulled up to the gates, the security guard appeared from behind a corrugated panel. He paused for a second, staring through the thick metal rails of the gate, and inside the van. He was delaying far too long for Davey's liking.

'What the fuck is he doing? Open the fucking gates, you fucking cockwomble.' The security guard couldn't hear him, and didn't appear moved to hasten his speed. Davey, left hand on the door handle, was just about to get out of the van when the guard signalled his intent to open the gates.

The padlock was removed, the heavy steel gates were manually opened, and the van drew alongside the guard.

'What the fuck are you doing? We haven't got time for no fucking beauty parade inspection. You're paid to open the gate, look the other way and do as you are fucking told.' Davey's tone was harsh, and again his voice was projecting louder and louder with each word uttered.

He reached inside his coat pocket and retrieved two buff envelopes, one distinctly fuller than the other.

'The top one is yours, and the bottom is for BJ. Don't get them mixed up, and make sure to give it to BJ when he calls on you.'

The security guard, for the first time finding some balls to stand his ground, said, 'alright, la, I'm not fuckin' stupid you know. Hurry the fuck up before the bizzies come sniffing around again.'

'Again?'

'Yeah, the bizzies have driven past two or three times in the last hour. You can generally go an entire shift without seeing any of them; although there was this one time, I was sat 'aving me scran...'

'Yeah, I'm not fucking bothered, just make sure you give that envelope to BJ.' And with that, the van pulled forward and started to make off into the distance with a clear purpose.

BJ was the local gangster, Liverpool's answer to the Kray twins; well, one of them anyway. Although if rumours were to be believed, he was vicious enough to be both Ronnie and Reggie combined. BJ, real name Barry Jacobs, owned Liverpool, not from an asset management or real estate perspective, but he owned the city's underbelly. BJ was 'top dog'; he controlled almost every element of major crime across the city. If he wasn't directly involved, then he had given his approval to those that were. BJ was aware of everything that went down in Liverpool, and many were the fools that had tried to circumvent his involvement or approval over the years, only to see themselves relieved of a finger or two as punishment for their lack of respect and understanding of 'how things worked'.

Jimmy Dolsen had been introduced to BJ just over nine years ago by a mutual friend. The timing, for Jimmy at least, was quite fortuitous as one of his transit routes into the UK had started to come under increased scrutiny from prying eyes, both at home and along the journey. UK Border Force and HM Revenue and Customs appeared to have invested in several additional cutters, and they all seemed to be patrolling the waters within which Jimmy's supply route was embedded. He had needed to make some changes.

Jimmy, like BJ, was a mass importer of Class A drugs. BJ had extended his import interests to include firearms and other weapons, but Jimmy had chosen to stick with what he knew, what he could move quickly, and what he could guarantee a sizeable profit on. Jimmy had expected their initial meeting to be somewhat awkward with both parties posturing, trying to demonstrate who the bigger man was. To Jimmy's surprise, he didn't find BJ to be like that at all. BJ knew that Jimmy was an importer, a drug dealer, a competitor, but he also knew that Jimmy would distribute only within the Greater Manchester area. Jimmy had openly stated that he had no interests in expanding his infrastructure into Liverpool, or any other areas where BJ might already be selling. BJ appeared to be relatively pragmatic about Jimmy's proposal; quite simply, the shipment would arrive at Liverpool docks, BJ would facilitate access into the shipyard, and allow the transportation of the drugs across Liverpool and back to Manchester. Not that anyone thought the transportation would be subject to a hijack attempt within the Liverpool area, but BJ also guaranteed the safety of the transport. For his part, BJ would receive a fat wad of notes each time a shipment arrived in the docks.

The van drove straight to where the container was to be found this time. It wasn't as though Liverpool dockyard was small by any means, but Davey Dolsen had been here twenty-five, maybe thirty times over the past three years alone. It would be fair to say, give Davey Dolsen a container location, and he'd find it in under five minutes.

The van was reversed up to the container doors, and the occupants alighted. Dolsen was pleased to see that the container he wanted was on the ground. As with most dockyards, the sturdy steel containers were generally stacked on top of each other, sometimes four or five high. Dolsen briefly recalled one visit last year where his lads had to scale two containers in order to reach the one they wanted, and they were less than impressed as it took them twice as long to offload into their van on that occasion.

The container was secured by two heavy duty steel padlocks, one at the top and one at the bottom of the door. Dolsen had brought an oxy-acetylene torch in the van in order to cut through the padlocks. A key would have been easier, but neither party, exporter or importer, could guarantee that the same container, and thus padlock, would be used for each shipment. As part of the support offered by BJ, he tasked the security guard with fitting two new padlocks to the container once Dolsen and his crew had left, disposing of the padlocks that had been cut through, and no-one was any the wiser.

'Okay, crack on, Terry.'

Terry opened the back doors of the van and retrieved the torch. The tanks were strapped to the inside wall of the van, and Terry turned the regulator and lit up the torch, and within less than a minute both padlocks had been cut like a knife through butter, and knocked off.

Within the container there were two wooden crates, their lids taking a matter of seconds to lever off with a crowbar. Davey, who until now had been supervising rather than doing, stepped forward and looked into the container. He reached deep inside one of them and retrieved a package about the size of a house brick. It was indeed a brick; a brick of pure cocaine.

35

Fifteen minutes later, Davey and his three crew had retrieved fifteen kilograms of cocaine and twenty kilograms of cannabis, and loaded them into the back of the van.

'That's it, Davey, we're all done.'

'Right, let's get crack on and get out of here. I fucking hate Liverpool.'

'It's alright actually, I've had some cracking nights out in Liverpool. The birds are fit; not a patch on Manchester though obviously. So, what's wrong with Liverpool, Davey?'

'It's full of fucking Scousers, that's what's wrong with Liverpool; they're fucking everywhere. The place is infested with them. Now then, la, go 'ed and get us an ale in before I go to me ma's for some scran.' Davey's all too authentic Scouse accent accompanied by his head and hand movements started chuckles of laughter reverberating through the van.

The journey back to and over the Greater Manchester border was quiet and uneventful, just as expected, and certainly just as they would have wanted when carrying thirty-five kilos of illegal drugs.

Davey's phone rang; it was Jimmy. The two wise heads knew better than to talk specifics over the phone.

'It's Jimmy.'

'I know, it comes up on my phone screen.'

'Knobhead.' There was a brief pause as Jimmy waited for Davey to respond. He didn't. 'Did you collect Aunty Marie from Liverpool?'

'We did, yes.'

'Is she okay?'

'Yes, in perfect form, as always. We have just arrived back now. I'll get her checked into the hotel, then I'll meet you for a beer.'

'Okay. Make sure that Aunty Marie is settled before you leave; don't leave it just to Terry.'

'Yes, Jimmy, I'll make sure that she's settled before I leave.'

The Dolsens had numerous places across Greater Manchester that they would use to temporarily store batches of drugs, either waiting to be bagged and distributed, or in the case of cocaine, waiting to be cut to about fifty percent purity before being bagged and then distributed.

Recently received shipments might be moved four or five times, as smaller batches, within the first few days after taking possession. Of course there was the added risk every time the batches were in transit; but the risk outweighed the possible alternative; a raid by the drug squad on one safe house, where most, if not all, of a recent shipment was being held. A large powerful gang they might be, but it would take several months to recover from a loss of that size, and that was assuming the loss of the drugs alone, and not any of the key members as well.

Aunty Marie was to be dropped off at an abattoir on St. Michael Street. The van pulled up outside the back doors, and after three bangs on the outside and a short wait, the door opened. It took less than five minutes to offload the thirty-five kilos into the abattoir. The back room was never used; a walk-in freezer, it had ten adult pigs suspended from hooks that were attached to a steel rail secured to the ceiling. The pigs, and the room itself, had a single purpose; to temporarily store the drugs for the Dolsens.

The abattoir owner, a portly Greek gentleman showing all of his fifty-nine years and more, was paid handsomely, not only for looking the other way and keeping quiet, and not only for the use of his walk-in freezer, but mainly for the three hours of activity that he would undertake after Davey had gone. He would wrap each brick in cellophane, and place them inside the gutted pigs. Once they were safely stashed inside, he would sew up the chest of the carcass, thus concealing the drugs until such time as they were needed again.

If the abattoir was ever visited by either the police, or more likely, the council environmental health officer, he would argue that the freezer in question was being used as a containment area for a bad batch of pigs that had disease, and they were awaiting collection to the incinerator. The story was plausible, and unlikely to initiate any further investigation from the environmental health officer, other than perhaps returning in seven days to ensure that the carcasses had actually been removed and incinerated. This could be arranged fairly easily by the abattoir owner, and without any hassle or paperwork confirming the suspected disease. Everyone was susceptible to a back-hander and some extra cash for looking the other way, or ticking a box on a form.

Either way, no-one was likely to want to cut open the carcasses of the pigs, thus revealing the drugs.

'Right, Terry, you sort the van and I'll give Tom a call to come and pick us up. I'll see you in a couple of hours.'

'Okay, Davey, will do.'

Terry now had a difficult job, and one that was made more difficult during daylight hours. He had to take the van, find somewhere remote, and torch it. Granted, this was not the most dangerous or taxing task within the world where they existed, but Jimmy had a rule that every time they used a vehicle for a major shipment collection; it had to be destroyed, and he meant *totally fucking destroyed; I don't even want anyone to know that it was a van, let alone pull any fucking fingerprints from it.* This approach generally cost them about three thousand pounds each time; but Jimmy was convinced that it was necessary, as retaining the same vehicle for multiple runs exponentially increased the chances of any drug residue in the vehicles, or the vehicles becoming known and tracked by the police. Add to which the driver, generally Terry, would have his fingerprints all over the vehicle. He could wear gloves, but *who the fuck wears gloves to drive,* Jimmy had noted; wearing gloves at the wheel of a vehicle was more likely to get you pulled by the police.

It was almost a full time job for Terry, buying and disposing of vehicles solely for the movement of drugs. He was helped in this regard by the local Romany community, gypsies. Their knowledge of vans for sale, for cash, was generally second to none. They even offered to 'relieve the owners' of their assets, for a modest fee of course, but Jimmy needed the vans to be road legal, and not registered as stolen. There literally was too much to lose. The more vehicles Terry had to dispose of, the harder it became to find suitable locations to dump and torch them. However, he was nothing if not creative.

CHAPTER 5

A re you ready, sergeant?' asked Priest, as he grabbed his jacket on the run. He neither waited for nor heard the reply to his somewhat rhetorical question, as he was out of the door and on his way to the car park. By the time he had reached his car, DS Baxter had caught him up, and they set off.

The road outside of the church and all those adjacent were already busy with parked cars; most of them, Priest assumed, were mourners attending the funeral. Baxter huffed, puffed and swore as it took him a good fifteen minutes to find a parking space, and even then the ten-minute walk back towards the church provided further opportunity for him to demonstrate his diverse vernacular of offensive language. Priest was unsure if and how his life would be enhanced by learning new words such as 'cockwomble' and 'knob-jockey', but he acknowledged that every day was a school day, and banked the phrases in the recesses of his brain.

'It's a good job that we arrived early then, sergeant,' Priest quipped.

As they neared the church and passed through the ornately carved wooden lychgate, Priest couldn't help but appreciate the picture postcard view in front of him. Yes, it was a relatively impressive and well preserved church from the late Norman period, but nothing too special, and nothing that you couldn't find in thousands of other towns and villages up and down the country. It was just after nine-thirty in the morning, and the mid-morning mist was clearly in a meteorological battle with the rising sun, neither of which wanting to give ground to the other. The outcome of which was a stunning hazy background with a powerful orange tint, an image which wouldn't have been out of place in any photograph of the year competition.

As they walked up the pea gravel footpath towards the entrance, Priest had noticed the heavy presence of what could only be referred to as private security, or gang members, as Priest clearly knew them to be. Security was expected to be tight at the funeral of one of the North West's most notorious drug dealers and gang leader. With someone having recently chopped the head off the snake, any rival gang with the balls to wipe out the balance of the top echelons of Yardie power in the North West only had to turn up in numbers spraying the mourners with a hail of bullets as they exited the church later that morning.

Priest and Baxter attracted a lot of attention as they walked towards the entrance door. Why? They were white, very white, and two weeks spent baking like a rotisserie chicken in the Spanish sun wasn't going to help them blend in to the wholly Afro-Caribbean attendees. Priest didn't mind, he wasn't there to blend in.

As expected, they were stopped at the door as one of the two security men stepped across their path. He was huge, his upper body doing its utmost to fill the doorframe, and that itself was bloody enormous. The man held out an outstretched arm.

'Is private, 'vitation only…and besides mi no let no babylon tru dees doors.'

The man's Caribbean patois was so deep, the only word that Priest caught was 'babylon', and he was all too familiar with that. Nevertheless Priest reached inside his jacket pocket and retrieved his warrant card; he unfolded the wallet cover and presented it, front and centre.

The man swatted it away, and spat on the ground. 'Move yuh bloodcleet fram yah suh.' He had swatted Priest's hand away with such force that his warrant card slipped out of his hand and to the ground. Baxter reacted immediately and started to square up to both of the security guards.

'It's okay, sergeant.'

'Yuh need fi guh nah,' said the second man with a softer undertone, but still an almost unrecognisable dialect to the two detectives.

Priest had resigned himself to the fact that they were not going to be granted access to the church, and they would need to wait outside for the duration of the service. That was until another man appeared from inside, and after uttering a single word, the two men parted to allow Priest and Baxter to enter. Priest didn't question it, nor did he get a chance to acknowledge his *permission* to enter. Inside they strolled.

The church was packed. Every seat on every long, narrow wooden pew was taken, with the exception of one at the rear, just long enough for two or three bums. Priest and Baxter made their way over and sat down.

The forty-five-minute service was an emotional affair, as all funerals generally are. Priest had spent most of that time tuned out to the hymns, the numerous kind words bestowed on the deceased, and the wails of crying from the female mourners, at times drowning out the eulogy and a surprisingly booming rendition of 'Amazing Grace'. Priest had been scanning the faces of the many mourners, mainly the men, and committing their faces to memory. Most of the mourners were, after all, part of the most notorious Yardie gang in the North West of England, and a rare opportunity presented itself to take stock of the many faces, both dons and soldiers, that might not be seen on a regular basis; certainly not all together in a single room.

That being said, funerals by their very nature are also family affairs, and the church pews were also full with children of all ages, some sitting quietly and in a mournful and reflective mood, other younger children, climbing on their parents' laps and generally being a handful.

It was fair to say that the church was awash with money; illegally attained money, but money nevertheless. Everyone was decked out in their finest attire, suited and booted in their Sunday best, to pay their last respects to the late Jarel Lamar Powell. Priest didn't dare think how many firearms were being carried and concealed at that very moment in time. He pondered for a second if it would be a wise move to call in a raid from the Tactical Firearms Unit, getting the firearms recovered and off the streets, no doubt resulting in the arrest and possible jail time for many of those sitting in close proximity to Priest. He pondered this briefly, despite the disrespect shown for the family at their time of mourning. The reality of that course of action would no doubt have been a bloody gun battle, and stand-off between two heavily armed groups; the police, outnumbered but highly skilled marksmen, trained to resist the urge of the trigger unless absolutely necessary. Whereas the other group were all too ready and eager to advance their gang reputation by killing a police officer, or two. No, despite Priest knowing that the church currently had enough firearms to start a coup in a small African country, he decided to brush it aside and refocus.

After the funeral service had ended, Priest and Baxter returned to their car, but not before halting at the lychgate and ensuring that they got a good look at every mourner, and every mourner had in turn clocked them.

The burial was to be held at High Moor Cemetery; Priest and Baxter not knowing this in advance had to follow the funeral cortege towards its destination.

High Moor was a council owned municipal cemetery, wide open in space with plenty of access, which presented the Yardie security team with an impossible task of restricting entry and ensuring the safety and security of the mourners. That being said, Priest had no intention of accompanying the mourners down at the graveside. He and Baxter stood a respectful distance away under a large horse chestnut tree, about one hundred metres from where the mourners had congregated. Their position was slightly elevated, and as such, served as a perfect vantage point upon which to continue scanning the crowd, and etching as many faces to memory as was possible.

The detectives watched for ten or fifteen minutes as the coffin was brought to the graveside, and various people appeared to take it in turns to speak, no doubt endowing the deceased, scum-bag drug dealer that he was, with narrative and sentiment about how generous and kind he was, or how a cute and loving child had matured into a family man with close social ties to the community.

From the corner of his right eye, Priest caught sight of two men who at first glance appeared to be doing much the same as he and DS Baxter were – standing a safe distance away, on an elevated position, keeping a watchful eye on the mourners. Only, one of the men had a camera. It was one of those cameras with a long lens, the kind that the paparazzi use, and the kind that appeared to protrude a good thirty centimetres from the camera itself, with a circumference of ten to fifteen centimetres. *It's a bloody big bugger,* Priest thought to himself; *he'll not be concealing that one down his jacket.* Priest nudged Baxter.

'Have you clocked those two over there?'

'Where?'

Priest pointed to the right. 'Two guys, one of them taking photos of the mourners.'

'Oh yes. I hadn't seen them before.' DS Baxter stared at the two men. Aside from the fact that they were at the funeral of a Yardie drug dealer taking photos of the mourners they appeared to be…well, just like Joe Public. Both were dressed in blue denim jeans and short coats, and one had fairly long unkempt hair, whilst the other had tight cropped hair but wore a heavy beard.

'What do you think, guv?'

'Well, they sure as hell don't look like gang members.' He paused for a second. 'I think they're police officers.'

'Really? Itchy and Scratchy over there, you must be joking?'

'Nope. Why don't you go over and introduce yourself?' asked Priest, 'go and find out who they are and what they are doing here.'

'Why?'

'Because I want to see their reaction when they know that we've clocked them.'

'You go then,' noted Baxter, in meek defiance.

'Errrr, me DCI…you DS….' and that pretty much ended that conversation.

Baxter started out towards them, and had covered roughly half of the ground before they noticed him briskly bearing down on their location. One of them picked up a rucksack from the floor and they both started a hasty retreat in the opposite direction. Baxter continued to run after them, but only as far as their original location, at which point he stopped. Knowing he wasn't the fittest or fastest officer on the force, he knew that he wasn't going to catch them.

Baxter turned towards Priest and shook his head. Priest, who had been watching with some amusement, acknowledged this with a brief laugh. It didn't matter; he knew who they were anyway.

The incident room was buzzing with noise; conversation, laughter, minor jovial disagreements and people moving around, swapping seats and quickly grabbing a coffee before the boss arrived.

Right on cue, DCI Priest walked through the doors to the incident room, together with the visitor whom he had just collected from the reception desk. They waded through the throngs of bodies sitting on chairs or perched on the edge of table tops, and positioned themselves at the front, next to the murder wall.

The commencement of his address was temporarily delayed as a uniformed officer handed Priest two cups of coffee, one of which he passed over to his visitor.

'Thank you.' He took a quick sip and placed it down on the adjacent table.

'Right, before I introduce our visitor, let's have a quick recap on our current situation, which in turn will shed some light on the reason that I have asked our visitor to join us today. Seven days ago, Jarel Lamar Powell was discovered in Oakwood Lane Woods just after eight-forty a.m. by a lady walking her dog. Mr Powell had been murdered. More specifically, it appears that he had been crucified, nailed to an oak tree. The pathologist confirmed that Mr Powell died from suffocation; not the type of suffocation that you and I might normally understand and be able to describe, but as the doctor noted, and I paraphrase for the purposes of time, the crucifixion led to significant breathing difficulties and he slowly suffocated, unable to get enough oxygen into his body.'

He paused to take a sip of coffee and smiled at his visitor briefly.

'Now, aside from this being a particularly brutal and unusual murder, the added dimension here is that Jarel Lamar Powell is, sorry was, the leader of the largest Yardie gang in the North West. Our initial hypothesis is that this is a gangland murder, some kind of turf war, or even retaliation for an as yet undiscovered murder of another gang member. We don't know; it's all a working hypothesis at the minute. What we do know for sure, however, is that we in our team here know next to nothing about the Yardie gangs in the North West. Yes we know they exist, and yes we know that they control an obscene amount of the drug trade, but what we don't know is anything about their members, their hierarchy, their gang rivals, their motivations, or to be honest, what the hell is going to happen next now that their top dog has been murdered.'

He paused for another sip of coffee, this time finishing off the contents. 'We…' he emphasised, 'don't know, but our visitor does.'

Finally after Priest's rambling introduction the assembled team would get to find out who their visitor was, who it had to be said, had displayed as much patience as the team had.

'I would like to introduce our visitor, Charles Mayfield.' Mayfield held up his hand and gave a brief smile. 'Mr Mayfield is a civilian contractor who has been working on a consultative basis for almost fifteen years, advising members of the multi-agency integrated gang management unit. He has an unrivalled knowledge of black gang culture in the North West of England, and specialises in Yardie gangs.' Priest gestured that the floor was his.

'Thank you, chief inspector.' Mayfield stepped forward. What he said next surprised a few, including Priest. 'If you haven't got a coffee, go and get one. I'll give you five minutes.'

No-one moved. A few heads turned towards Priest, who gestured his approval, but even then not a soul moved.

'Okay,' said Mayfield, 'let's crack on. Detective Chief Inspector Priest has asked me along today, to help provide some insight that might be useful to you all over the course of your investigation. Over the next sixty minutes I am going to share my knowledge; well some of my knowledge, and some facts and figures around black gang culture. Make no mistake; some of this knowledge will be a prerequisite to gaining some traction in your investigation. Yardie gang culture is a closed door; you will never get close enough to understand the soldiers, let alone the leaders. You're not investigating the murder of a middle-class guy in white suburbia; this is the murder of the highest general in the Yardie gang outside of London, and when the Yardies commence their retaliation, and they will, it is likely to rain fucking fire over Manchester for months and months.'

DC Simkins leant over to Baxter. 'This is a bit over dramatic, don't you think?' Baxter didn't hear him, he was already formulating his own words that passed his lips just as Simkins had finished.

'There are some seasoned detectives in this room, Mr…?'

'Mayfield.'

'Mayfield, yes. As I was saying, there are some experienced detectives sitting amongst us, myself included, and we have investigated our fair share of murder over the last few years, some of it gang related.'

'Sergeant.' Priest stepped in with a single word of caution, knowing that Baxter could veer off in any direction with his points of view, all of which were likely to be less than diplomatic.

'It's okay, chief inspector,' advised Mayfield, 'sergeant, let me ask you a question or two.'

'Okay.' Baxter sat upright in his chair, ready for whatever was to be thrown at him.

'How many Yardie gang members have been murdered in the last twelve months?' Baxter didn't really see the relevance of the question, and shook his head.

'How many Yardie gang members are there within a ten-mile radius of this police station?' Again, Baxter shook his head.

'Which gang, or gangs, are the Yardies' fiercest rivals in the North West?' No response from Baxter. 'You see, sergeant; I have no doubt that you are a capable and experienced team of detectives, but you know absolutely nothing about Yardie gangs. And that would most certainly be your Achilles heel.'

Priest stepped in once again. 'Let's get back on track if we can?'

Despite his obvious maturing years, Charles Mayfield still unconsciously projected himself as an imposing figure. His long greying dreadlock hair and jet black skin gave away his Caribbean heritage if not his actual birthplace. Whereas the facial scars, especially the one that extended from his mouth to his lower eyelid, did little to hide the secret that he was no stranger to violence, if not directly involved in a gang in some form or another in years gone by.

'Let me start by telling you something about this Yardie crew that has been right on your doorstep for longer than most of you have been alive. The crew, of which Jarel Lamar Powell was the head, is said to be some five hundred strong right now. The hierarchy will consist of a core of around fifty key members who will either be Jamaican born, or direct descendants of Jamaican nationals, no more than second generation in the U.K. These are what you would refer to as Yardies. Yardie gangs have a live-for-today philosophy, by that I mean that they have little or no money laundering or investment infrastructure. Newer, younger members tend to spend money and live well, whereas older members will still send thousands of pounds back to their families in Jamaica every month. This makes it difficult to follow any structured money trail, and damn near impossible to tie them down to any Al Capone style income or tax charges.'

He paused for a brief second to make sure everyone was still with him. They were.

'Outside of that core fifty, the Yardies have an extended reach of a further three hundred, perhaps up to four hundred and fifty members through affiliations with gangs you will no doubt have heard of; the Moss Side Crew, Longsight Crew and the New Hulme Boyz as an example of just three. These affiliates are gangs in their own right, but are all British born hoodlums easily influenced by the Jamaican elders and Yardie generals. When the Yardies demand their support, these affiliate gang members will dance to their tune. You will be surprised how many crimes perpetrated by gangs in the North West are actually doing the bidding of the Yardies. My guess is that over sixty percent of the crimes that have been, or will be, associated with other North West, predominantly black, gangs will actually be carried out at the behest of the Yardies.'

Mr Mayfield took a breather, before continuing. His audience was now in the main hanging on his every word, intrigued by tales of this network of violent criminals and gangsters, that by all accounts had dominated the belly of Greater Manchester's underworld for decades, and had done so without getting as much as a single parking ticket between them all.

'Jamaicans have been flocking in their thousands to this country for decades; there was a significant influx in the fifties and sixties when cheap low skilled labour was required. This influx of labour, you will no doubt be aware, was known as the Windrush generation, named retrospectively after the ship HMT Empire Windrush that brought the first West Indian immigrants, back in 1948. Here in the UK this new labour was quickly labelled as Yardies due to their lower financial and social status, and in direct comparison to the social housing projects back in Jamaica where most of them originated from. You may have heard the term 'government yards', immortalised in Bob Marley lyrics for example. Anyway, the poverty, crime and violence became endemic in those neighbourhoods, leading to the occupants being stigmatised by the term Yardie. As these immigrants settled in London, the behaviours and gang violence were clearly not shed with their move to their new surroundings, and the wider British public soon further saw fit to stigmatise the behaviour of the whole Jamaican immigrant community as Yardie culture.'

Brief pause, and a quick check that his audience was still with him. They were.

'We believe that the London community started to dilute at around this point, and there is evidence that relatively large groups of Jamaican immigrants moved to northern areas of the country, most notably to Nottingham and Manchester.'

'Any reason as to why those two cities?' piped up one young constable.

'That's a good question, and I wish I had a good answer for you, but I don't. Sorry. I can't give you a definitive answer as to why Nottingham and Manchester were fortunate enough to receive an influx of such a formidable and utterly terrifying group of individuals.

'Anyway, most of the police forces up and down the country have historically been hesitant to categorise Yardies as organised gangs, as there appeared to be no real structure or leadership. Both of which, it has been argued, are prerequisites for a gang, or a group of individuals, to be categorised as 'organised'. We know for definite that your man Jarel Lamar Powell was at the helm and controlled the operation across the North West, but there doesn't appear to be a known or recognised structure beneath him. We see the Yardies as a gang that operates with a splintered structure; highly organised but with a hierarchy that probably remains relatively fluid, aside from the top man himself that is.'

Over the course of the next twenty minutes, Mr Mayfield went on to impart some of his knowledge on topics ranging from the type of drugs that the Yardies controlled, and conversely those that they would generally stay clear of; the weapons of choice for this ultra-violent gang which no doubt had a direct bearing on their average life expectancy of just thirty-five, and finally his own thoughts on the impending and inevitable retribution for the murder of Jarel Lamar Powell.

After a brief question and answer session, Charles Mayfield was escorted back to reception by a uniformed officer, and the assembled team started to chat amongst themselves for a few minutes before order was called by DCI Priest.

'So, what did we think to what Mr Mayfield had to say?' There was a brief pause as Priest waited for some interaction and engagement from his team. Nothing. 'I thought it was very interesting in a general manner, but from a more specific level, personally I thought that his insight into Yardie gang culture will hopefully play a big part in helping us navigate through this case.'

'Navigate,' said Baxter under his breath towards Simkins, 'what the fuck is he talking about, navigate.'

'It means…' Simkins was cut short.

'I know what it fucking means, muppet.'

'So, quick recap on where we are and we'll call it a day,' Priest noted with a quick glance at his wristwatch.

'Our victim is Jarel Lamar Powell, a black male, aged forty-two. Married to Delanna Powell with two young boys, and lives in a smart residential area just off Maine Road. Powell was discovered in Oakwood Lane Woods seven days ago by a woman walking her dog at approximately eight forty-two, clearly having been murdered. The two elements that make this case somewhat different to any we may have encountered in the past are; firstly our victim appears to have been crucified, nailed to a tree in what, to me at least, appears to be a clear message to his enemies. And secondly, following on from the message to the enemies, it would appear that our victim was the leader of the largest Yardie gang in the North West, and it seems logical that we could have a gangland murder on our hands. The reason for which we don't currently know, so we have a lot of work to do in a very short space of time. No forensics were recovered from the body, and whilst we wait on potential forensics from the crime scene itself, the very fact that more people trampled through that area than is seen on a busy Saturday at Manchester's Piccadilly train station leaves me with little hope of anything useful.' Priest took a breath.

'So, let's get our thinking caps on, people. Why was Powell murdered? Was it a revenge attack? Was it gang or drug related? Was it his gang enemies, or perhaps one of his own gang that murdered him? Will anyone benefit from his murder? If so, who and why? If it was a revenge attack, we need to be looking at all unsolved murders over the past three, possibly six months to try and find a link. I want a preliminary list of suspects, or some educated thoughts at least, within twenty-four hours.'

With Priest still standing at the front adjacent to the murder wall, but with an elongated period of silence filling the room, the team assumed that the briefing was over and they started to stand up and disperse.

'Get a good night's rest,' Priest noted, 'tomorrow's going to be a hell of a day.' Some of the experienced detectives smiled inwardly and winced at his choice of words, whereas the more junior constables appeared more confused at his sign-off statement.

CHAPTER 6

A re you off home, Vicky?' The passing male enquirer didn't receive a verbal reply, but rather a sharp scowl and a look of frustration mixed with anger that was in some part fuelled by the high level consumption of alcohol that night, together with the fact that she hated being called Vicky. Her name was Victoria, and everyone knew it. It wasn't as though she was a stranger in the Zanzibar nightclub.

It was four a.m. and the club had started to die down significantly over the last thirty or forty minutes, so Victoria Dolsen had decided it was time to leave, and go home.

'Get my coat will you, babe?' The recipient of this request was Victoria's boyfriend, Johannes De Groot.

'Yeah, sure. Are you waiting here, or coming over?'

'I'll follow you over in a minute,' she replied, as she picked up the champagne flute and finished the last drop of the Veuve Clicquot that she and Johannes had been quaffing all evening, interspersed with the house speciality champagne cocktail, Black Velvet, a marriage of the upper class champagne mixed with the working class of the Guinness. It was a cocktail that the club owner had said summed up the club perfectly.

As Victoria moved towards the exit, she saw the owner talking to a couple of young women. As she approached, the two women took a pace backwards as if to let her closer to him. His name was James Dolsen, her brother.

Victoria moved in and kissed James on the cheek. 'I'm off home, James.'

'Okay, sweetheart. You had a good night?'

'Always. You know me.'

'Hmmm, probably too much of a good night then. Have I still got any champagne left behind the bar?'

'Of course you have, James,' she chuckled, 'well...I think you have.' She leant inward and kissed him again, which was swiftly followed by a hug.

James Dolsen wasn't to be seen in the club very often, and Victoria hadn't seen him for a few weeks. She however, was a regular at the Zanzibar. Most Saturday nights she could be found in the VIP area, either with Johannes, or with any number of her girlfriends.

'Alright, stay safe. Is Johannes taking you home?'

'Yes.'

Victoria navigated her way down two flights of stairs, as gingerly as she could noting her five-inch heels, and considering she was a couple of drinks beyond what could generally be described as *pissed as a fart*. She rounded the corner, and Johannes was there waiting, with coat in hand.

'There you are. What have you been doing?'

'Just talking to James, babe, just talking to James.' She turned her back to him, and he duly obliged by placing her coat over her shoulders. She grabbed his hand, interlocked fingers, and they walked towards the front door.

One of the door staff broke off his conversation to step forward and open the door for them. 'Goodnight, Miss Dolsen.'

She flashed him a smile. 'Night, Paul, see you next week.'

'Of that I have no doubt,' he replied. Her boyfriend didn't quite receive the same cordial verbal engagement, although his presence was acknowledged with a nod of the head in his general direction as he passed behind Victoria.

After ensuring Victoria now had both arms inside her black faux fur coat, Johannes reached inside his jacket and retrieved a pack of cigarettes and a lighter. He placed two cigarettes in his mouth and proceeded to light them both before handing one to Victoria.

'Paul, be a darling and call us a taxi will you, babe?'

Again, Paul left his half-finished conversation to attend to Victoria. 'Yeah, sure. Where are you gonna be? Are you hanging around here?'

'Yes, thank you.'

Paul disappeared inside for a few minutes and reappeared just as he returned his mobile phone back to his pocket. 'It'll be about fifteen minutes, Victoria.'

'Fifteen minutes…' she bellowed with a disproportionate level of disgust considering that it was only the waiting time for a taxi, and not the total timeline within which she would be tortured by having her fingernails extracted with a pair of rusty pliers.

'Okay, can you call them back and say that we are going to start walking up Bale Street, and that we'll probably meet them outside that noodles place?'

'Oodles?'

'Yes, Oodles of Noodles. Stupid name for a food joint if you ask me.' And with that they started to walk off, Johannes' arm outstretched over her shoulder, pulling her in tight from the early morning chill.

'Next time I see James, babe, remind me to tell him that he needs to buy a taxi company.'

'Let me guess; should he always have a spare car on standby every weekend to bring you back home when you've finished partying?'

'Correct.'

'You don't need a taxi, babe, you just need a chauffeur.'

'We need a chauffeur, babe; you know I don't go anywhere without you.'

Walking hand in hand, occasionally leaning in to gently kiss each other, Victoria and Johannes meandered slowly up the road, watched periodically by Paul the doorman until they disappeared out of sight. As they rounded the corner into Bale Street, ahead some two hundred metres they could see a taxi parked up on the left-hand side of the road, right outside the noodle shop. Neither of them moved to quicken their pace. The taxi would wait for them; *she was Victoria Dolsen.*

Neither of them heard the car slowly drawing up behind them; that was until it started to gather speed over the last twenty metres before screeching to a halt adjacent to where they were standing. The braking noise was sufficient for their hearts to miss a beat, until they realised the car had stopped on the road, and wasn't about to plough into them.

The front and rear passenger side windows were already down when the black SUV came to a halt; and leaning out of the window were two men, each holding a Mach-10 sub-machine pistol. Without hesitation or delay both men opened fire on the pedestrians, spraying bullets in their direction. They only relented when both magazines were empty, which was the cue for the car to pull away again at high speed.

Both Victoria and Johannes had been hit. With Victoria walking closest to the road, she appeared to have received the most gunshot wounds. They both fell down heavily onto the pavement, and Victoria's body lay lifelessly across her boyfriend's chest as the pavement started to stain with a covering of cardinal red blood.

The taxi driver, only some twenty metres ahead, had witnessed the whole thing through his rear view mirror, although the incident took little more than three or four seconds from the screeching halt to the high speed exit. He exited his car, and ran towards the back where he stood motionless for a few seconds. He was shocked and scared, for sure, and he was unsure what to do. For a second he thought about simply driving off, after all, this wasn't the kind of thing that he wanted to get wrapped up in: police statements, identity parades, giving evidence in court, witness protection, harassment, death threats......death; his own, his family's.

Then he briefly thought about what would be the right thing to do: call an ambulance, call the police, and perhaps try and help the young couple lying on the floor, with blood oozing from their bodies as every second passed by.

Fuck that, he thought to himself. The magnitude of the situation and his own self-preservation was outweighing any civic or moral duty he had at this point in time; four a.m. on Bale Street on a Saturday night.

No, fuck that, he reaffirmed his last thought. He got back into his car and drove off.

'I'm sure I've said this before,' remarked DC Simkins just as DCI Priest came into earshot, 'but I wish people wouldn't get murdered in the middle of the bloody night. It seriously interferes with my sleep, and I need a good eight hours every night.' He exaggerated a yawn to make his point.

'When would you like them to get murdered, Robert?' Priest asked somewhat sarcastically, and clearly not expecting an answer.

'Well, guv, if I arrive at the station just before eight in the morning, perhaps give me an hour or so to get a couple of coffees down my neck, a chance to catch up on the banter from the previous evening, perhaps read the morning paper; so shall we say around eleven, guv?'

'Eleven it is then, Robert. Do you think on this occasion, however, that you can drag your arse into gear and support the investigation with this one, and then I'll wave my magic wand for you, and ensure that all future murders in the North West of England occur Monday to Friday around eleven o'clock in the morning.'

'Perfect, guv, perfect.'

DS Baxter clipped Simkins around the back of the head as he walked past him. 'Dickhead.'

DCI Priest walked over to the area sealed off by crime scene tape, and towards one of the uniformed constables.

He was accompanied by Baxter walking behind, and Simkins, slightly ahead. Simkins appeared to be walking with some discomfort.

'Are you alright, Robert?'

'Yes, guv, why do you ask?'

'Well, to be honest, and at the risk of being blunt, you look like you have shit yourself.'

'I had a curry last night, guv, and I've got an arse like the Japanese flag.' It took Priest a few seconds to connect the two. Simkins continued, 'one of those chicken phalls. Have you ever had a phall? Fucking hell, guv, it's hotter than...'

Priest didn't let him finish. 'Yes, Robert, we've got the idea; hot curry, arse on fire, suffering this morning.'

'Yes, guv.'

Priest turned his attention to the uniformed officer. 'No doctor yet?'

'No, guv, he's not arrived yet.'

'Okay, what do we have?'

'Two victims, one female still in situ. She's dead, I'm afraid. The other victim, a male, was still alive when we arrived so he's on his way to the hospital.'

'Okay, hang on a second.' Priest turned towards the other detectives, waiting patiently a few metres behind him. 'We have a male victim, still alive and on his way to hospital. Can one of you make your way up there and report back on his status? Let's try and speak to him before he goes into surgery.'

DC Simkins looked at DS Baxter, who returned the stare. Whilst it might seem a relatively cushy job, Baxter had no intention of sitting in the hospital for the next few hours suffering mind-numbing boredom until the victim came out of surgery, assuming he made it to surgery in the first place. 'Go on then, Robert, it sounds like a task with your name on it.'

Returning to the uniformed officer, Priest asked, 'anything else of interest, constable? Any witnesses, by any chance.'

'No, sir, not as far as we can tell. The emergency call was made by a taxi driver shortly after four-thirty this morning. He's still over there, sitting in his taxi if you want a word.'

'Thank you.'

Priest chose not to take a closer look at the female victim on the pavement, although there wasn't much that he couldn't deduce from the bloodstained body that lay motionless on the pavement.

'Ah, Detective Chief Inspector Priest.' The police doctor had arrived. 'What do you have for me this early morning?'

Priest looked over his shoulder towards the blood-splattered body of the female. 'It's all yours, doctor; I'll be back in ten or fifteen minutes.'

'Okey dokey.'

Okey fucking dokey. Priest inwardly chuckled at the outdated response, but then immediately recalled the song by Merle Haggard, 'Okie from Muskogee'; *I'm proud to be an Okie from Muskogee, a place where even squares can have a ball, we still wave Old Glory down at the courthouse, and white lightnin's still the biggest thrill of all.* He wasn't happy. The song would be in his head for the rest of the day now; and he hated, really hated country music. His hatred stemmed from his youth, when his parents used to play twelve-inch vinyls of Merle Haggard, Willie Nelson, Tammy Wynette and Hank Williams around the house all day long. These sessions of prolonged torture were occasionally peppered with interludes of Johnny Cash and Garth Brooks, which Priest actually found to be slightly less intolerable. Such prolonged exposure to a specific music genre was always going to send an impressionable Jonny Priest one way or the other; either towards being a fully paid up member of the country and western appreciation society, or as actually happened, a member of the listening audience asking *what is this shit that is making my ears bleed?*

Priest made his way over to the taxi driver, where he found DS Baxter already with him.

'Guv, this is Mohammed Akthar; he was the gentleman that made the 999 call.'

'Mr Akthar, sorry for the inconvenience, we'll try not to keep you for too long. Can you tell me the events leading up to the 999 call please?' asked Priest.

Mohammed Akthar took a long drag on his cigarette. 'Okay, well it's as I told the other policeman, I was driving up this road to collect my next fare on Jocelyn Street, when I noticed something on the pavement. As I got closer, I saw that it was a couple of people; at first I thought they must be drunk and had fallen down. To be honest I wouldn't normally have stopped, but as I drew up alongside them, I could see the blood all over the pavement, so I called for an ambulance.'

'Did you see anyone else around? Walking away, or perhaps any other cars?'

'No, the street was empty. There are very few people around at this time of night. I generally work the night shift at a weekend, and at this time it's generally the night club stragglers, and they are few and far between. You tend to be busy around two o'clock with the usual clubs and late bars, then it quietens off until about seven or eight when those rave-type clubs start to empty.'

'Okay, thanks. Can you give your statement to my colleague please? We might need to talk to you again in the next day or two.'

'Okay, not a problem.'

Priest turned and walked back toward the crime scene and engaged the SOCO officer. 'Any early findings?'

'Still early days, sir, but so far we've recovered forty-six shell casings; they look like a nine millimetre to me.'

'Forty-six, bloody hell, that's a lot of bullets. Are you sure?' He interrupted himself as he knew it was a stupid question that directly challenged the officer's capability and professionalism, let alone his ability to count. 'Sorry, of course you're sure.'

'Yes, sir. I think it had to be two guns. Either that or a single gun with a large clip, say thirty-two rounds that was reloaded. It sounds like a lot of bullets, and for a shooting it is a lot, but you can dispatch a thirty-two round clip in about three seconds. So if you factor in the time to change the magazine, a single shooter could have done this in; well, I dunno, about ten seconds.'

'Thank you, that's really useful, constable…'

'Peters, sir, Constable Peters.'

'Thank you.'

'For what it's worth, guv, and sorry, you'll know far more than me, but I find it highly unlikely that the shooter would choose to reload after emptying thirty-two bullets into his victims. I'm sure thirty-two would be enough in anyone's world. So my guess would err on the side of two shooters, sir.'

'I tend to agree. Thank you again, constable.'

Priest turned toward the police doctor, Doctor Bell. 'Any early thoughts yourself, doctor?'

'Well, she has been shot.' They shared a smile; the sarcasm and brevity wasn't lost on Priest.

'At the minute, I can see fifteen, possibly sixteen entry wounds, although I'm still counting as I find, and exact confirmation will be easier back at the mortuary when we can remove all the clothing. She's a real mess, chief inspector, a real mess.'

'I know, poor girl.'

Priest rounded up his team and advised them to go home and get some sleep, as tomorrow, or today as it actually was already, was going to be a busy day. 'See you in the office at nine,' he said.

Baxter looked at his watch. It was already six-thirty, and by the time he got back home it would be close to seven-thirty; assuming he needed an hour to get showered, dressed and drive to work, that left thirty minutes for sleep, even if he were to drop off as soon as his head hit the pillow.

'Fuck it, I'll go back to the office,' he announced.

Priest looked at his watch, and quickly made the same calculations in his head. 'Are you sure?'

Baxter thought about walking Priest through his timeline, but quickly decided that he couldn't be bothered. 'Yes, I'm sure.'

'Good man, I'll join you. Who needs sleep anyway?'

Fifteen minutes into the drive back to the police station, Priest's mobile phone awakened to the sonorous ringtone that is Wagner's 'Ride of the Valkyries'.

'Priest,' he answered with his usual crispness.

'Guv, it's Simkins.'

'Yes, Robert, how is our guy in the hospital?'

'Not good to be honest, guv. We have an ID from his wallet; his name is Johannes De Groot. The doctor confirmed that he appears to have been shot seven times, and he is now in surgery. Going to be a long one, guv; I don't see him coming out of surgery for the next four to five hours.'

'Okay. I don't suppose you managed to speak to him first, did you?'

'No, guv, he was unconscious upon arrival, and remained that way until they wheeled him into surgery about ten minutes ago.'

'Fuck! I hope he makes it through. Anyway, go home, Robert and try and get some sleep. Let's regroup at the station tomorrow morning.'

'It is tomorrow morning, guv. It's six forty-five.'

'Good point. The rest of the team are heading straight to the station. Feel free to join us, or go home for a couple of hours, Robert, I'm easy either way.'

'I'll probably just head in, guv, if that's alright.'

'Okay, I'll see you there.'

CHAPTER 7

I t was a little after eight when DS Stephens strode through the doors of the incident room. She hadn't been one of the team called out to the shooting earlier that morning. Well, to be fair she had been called, but Priest had abused his position somewhat and told her to stay in bed; which would have been fine had he not kept her awake for the following fifteen to twenty minutes as he crashed, banged, rattled and generally made more noise than a one-man band with a penchant for a double harmonica, and a pair of twelve-inch cymbals strapped to his knees.

'Good morning, Nic.'

'Morning, Jonny. Have you been at it since four-thirty?'

'Pretty much, yes. We finished up at the scene about six-thirty, and I thought it was a waste of time going home for what would be little more than half an hour.'

'Did everyone else share your enthusiasm and dedication?' Stephens said, looking around at the sparsely populated room.

'They did actually. Well, it was only myself, Baxter and Simkins, but yes they came straight into the station from the scene, although Robert returned separately from the hospital.'

'Hospital; why, what's wrong with him?'

Priest laughed, 'nothing, you muppet. I sent him to the hospital to follow up on the boyfriend that was alive when the ambulance crew arrived, and took him back to hospital. I was hoping that Robert might catch him for a few words before he went into surgery.'

'And?'

'No such luck; he was unconscious when he arrived, and remained so until he was wheeled into the operating theatre.'

'I hope he pulls through.'

'Me too, Nic, me too. It's a long shot, forgive the pun, but he might be able to provide us with a description; the vehicle, the shooters, anything.'

'So, where is everyone then?'

'Baxter and Simkins are having some breakfast in the canteen, as are a couple of the attached uniforms that were with us this morning.'

Right on cue, half a dozen officers filed through the door behind them. Added to the five already in the room, almost a full complement.

Priest walked over to the murder wall, which had been split down the middle and new information added.

'Right, morning, all. As of earlier this morning we now have two murders and an attempted murder. On the left you will all be familiar with Jarel Lamar Powell discovered in Oakwood Lane Woods ten days ago, and had been cru-cified on a large oak tree. Powell, we understand to be the leader of the one of the North West's largest Yardie gangs, controlling a large slice of the illegal drug supply in the area. Common sense would tell us that this is a gangland killing, perhaps a revenge killing, but we don't know for sure at this point in time.'

Priest took a step back and pointed towards the latest edition to the wall, saying, 'this is new. Here we have Victoria Dolsen and her boyfriend Johannes De Groot, both of whom were shot multiple times earlier this morning by, as yet, persons unknown. Victoria died at the scene, and Johannes is currently in surgery at the Royal Manchester Infirmary. Apparently it will be a bloody miracle if he pulls through as I understand he took seven bullets.'

He could see a couple of the officers straining their eyes at both pictures. 'Yes, sorry about the quality of the photos, these are the best we could get in the last hour or so.' Priest regarded the grainy images on the wall, a mixture of pulling the driving licence photo for both, coupled with a poor quality print from an office printer that was clearly in need of a toner replenishment. Neither had been in the custody of the police before; neither had previous identification photos in the system.

'Victoria Dolsen, guv,' piped up DC Wright, 'I've seen her a few times in some of the clubs. Isn't she the sister of...'

'Yes,' interjected Priest before she completed her question, 'she is the sister of Jimmy Dolsen, another one of Manchester's prominent scumbags, purportedly another of the area's major drug distributors.'

'Are we linking the two murders, guv?'

'We are, Stacey, yes, although somewhat tenuously. There is no direct link at the present time, although I can't help feeling that the murder of a major drug dealer, shortly followed by the murder of a close family member of a competing drug gang, is not a coincidence.'

'Let the scumbags wipe each other out, I say.'

'Thank you for that, DC Simkins. Whilst I've no doubt that most people share your view to a certain degree, we have a job to prevent such things happening on the streets of Greater Manchester. Add to which, it isn't clear at present if Victoria Dolsen was engaged any some capacity in Jimmy's drug empire, or if she was just an innocent victim, and perceived guilty by association.'

'Guv.'

'Incidentally, how are our Japanese friends?'

The room was oblivious to the context behind the question, which was probably just as well for Simkins.

'Yeah, getting better I think, guv. Thanks for asking.' Priest smiled.

'DS Stephens and I are going to see Jimmy Dolsen. DS Baxter will manage the lines of enquiry for Powell, and DS Grainger will do likewise for the Dolsen murder, and the De Groot attempted murder. There is a list of two dozen things we need to be cracking on with, so I suggest we do just that; crack on.'

'Am I driving, or you?' asked Stephens.

'Do you know where we are going?'

'No.'

'There you go then, that's cleared that one up.' Priest smiled at her. Her retort was more of a smirk.

James 'Jimmy' Dolsen lived in a nice five-bedroom detached Georgian-style house in Salford. Nothing too flash, and nothing too overtly extravagant, just like Jarel Powell. Most of the cars parked on the private driveways or roadside were high end: Mercedes, BMW, and Range Rover. Not that he would know himself, but he shared his immediate neighbourhood with a number of relatively high net worth middle-class individuals: doctors, accountants, company directors of this, business owners of that. It was the high end, brand new Range Rovers that clearly identified Dolsen's house. When Priest and Stephens arrived there were two on the driveway and a further two parked on the roadside.

Priest parked behind the rear Range Rover, and he and Stephens exited to walk towards the house; as they did both kerbside doors of the front vehicle opened and two men alighted.

'Can we help you?' said the first guy, clearly making reference to the fact that they came as a pair, and they would need to deal with them both.

'No, I don't think so. We're here to see your boss.'

The first guy stood his ground as Priest tried to pass him. 'I think you're in the wrong place. Can I suggest that you leave?'

Priest reached inside his jacket and extracted his warrant card.

'Detective Chief Inspector Priest, and like I said, we are here to see James Dolsen.'

For a second time, the guy stood his ground and refused to let them pass. 'Like I said, officer, I think you're in the wrong place.'

'Look, dickhead, if I were to seize and search these four very nice high class motors here, what are the chances do you think of finding any illegal firearms, or perhaps the sniffer dogs will pick up on some drug residue? Either way, I'll find a way to impound all four of them for at least six months. I'm not here for that shit, well not today anyway, now be good little boys, and fuck off out of my way.' That appeared to do the trick.

As they approached the doorstep, a man opened the door and stepped over the threshold to meet them.

'Cops?'

'Yes, Detective Chief Inspector Priest, and this is Detective Sergeant Stephens. And you are?'

'Jimmy, Jimmy Dolsen. And what can I do for Manchester's finest?'

Jimmy Dolsen wasn't at all what Priest expected, although he hadn't really any preconceived ideas on what a drug dealer at the top of his game might look like. Dolsen wasn't a spring chicken, but then he hadn't reached middle age either, and looked as expected for his thirty-eight years. At five foot nine, give or take, he wasn't dominant in stature, nor did he project an aura of aggression or dominance. He was dressed smart casual, in quality denim jeans and a white Lacoste polo shirt buttoned to the top, complemented by a pair of brown suede desert boots.

'Mr Dolsen. First of all, please accept our condolences for the loss of your sister. Please rest assured that we are doing everything we can to find and apprehend those responsible.'

'Don't worry, chief inspector, we know who is responsible.'

'Really? Then you need to come forward and share the information with us.'

'Yeah, that's not how things work in our world, is it?'

'I would urge against any kind of revenge attack, Mr Dolsen.'

'I'm sure you would, that's your job.'

'We have already had one murder recently. Do you know Jarel Powell, Mr Dolsen?'

'Who?'

'Jarel Powell?'

'Sorry, can't say that I do. Who is he?'

'Who was he? He was found murdered ten days ago, and we have reason to believe that his murder was gang related.'

'Gangs? Ah, you mean like the Bloods and the Crips from the mean streets of Los Angeles. Those kinds of gangs?' His sarcasm wasn't lost on either Priest or Stephens, nor did it resonate as mildly humorous.

'No, I mean like the Moss Side Crew, the Longsight Crew, or the New Hulme Boyz, or…' he hesitated for a second for effect, 'perhaps the Dolsen family.'

Jimmy Dolsen started to laugh with a noise that was as artificial as it was annoying. 'The Dolsen family?' cue further laughing, 'oh, chief inspector, you've made my day. I can't believe that you would think that my family and I, entrepreneurs one and all, would be a, a gang. Hilarious, bloody hilarious. Wait until I tell our Davey, he'll piss himself.'

'Hmmm, not literally I hope?' Priest's comment went straight over his head. 'So, Mr Dolsen, can you tell me where you were on the fourteenth of April?'

'Of course, I was here, at home.'

'How can you be so sure? It was ten days ago, and I haven't even asked you what time.'

'I've got an exceptionally good memory, me, chief inspector, a good memory. Oh, and I was at home all day.'

'And I suppose…' Priest was cut short.

'Yes, I have plenty of people that will confirm that to you. Shall we go inside and ask them?' Dolsen pointed towards his open front door.

As tempted as Priest was to get a look inside Dolsen's house, he didn't actually expect to get past the front door. Dolsen, no doubt, would stand at the front door and shout for his entourage to come outside.

'No, thank you, Mr Dolsen. We've got all we need for now, but I'm sure that we will be back. Don't leave town, eh?'

Don't leave town; what the bloody hell was that? Priest silently berated himself as he couldn't quite understand what possessed him to say such a stupid, cringe-worthy, outdated and moronic statement. They returned to the car, Priest started the engine and DS Stephens started to laugh.

'Don't leave town.'

'Don't, please, don't. I've literally got no fucking idea why I said that. It seemed like a good idea a couple of minutes ago.'

'Oh, Jonny, you are funny.'

'I'm glad that I bring a smile to your face, Nic.'

'For an experienced senior officer, you do come out with some shit sometimes, Jonny.'

'I'm here to please, Nic, I'm here to please.'

Priest had been back at the station barely thirty minutes when the call came down from Margaret Priddy; Superintendent Sawden wanted to see him, in his office.

After exchanging pleasantries with Margaret, Priest strode into Sawden's office.

'Ah, Priest. Finally.'

Finally, Priest thought, *you only bloody called me five minutes ago.* 'Yes, sir, I came as quick as I could.'

Priest turned to look at the visitor in Sawden's office, expecting an introduction, which he duly received.

'Chief inspector, this is Inspector Coker from the Serious Organised Crime Agency.' Priest stepped forward and the two shook hands.

'What can we do for SOCA, inspector?'

'I understand that you met with Jimmy Dolsen earlier today. Can I ask what you talked about, and why you were there?'

'Bloody hell, that was fast, I've been back at the station less than an hour. How did you....' Priest stopped himself. 'You have an undercover officer in Dolsen's gang, don't you? Placed where? Doing what? Who is it?'

'Clearly I can't divulge too many details, save to say that we have had a guy undercover for the past thirteen months. He has been predominately working as a bouncer in some of the pubs and clubs that the Dolsen family own, but has also been steadily and successfully gaining the trust of the family, and getting more involved in the family business.'

'If you have had a guy undercover for thirteen months, surely you have gathered enough evidence to charge them by now?'

'Yes, and no. Sure, we have gathered enough evidence to lock up plenty of the foot soldiers for a few years apiece maybe, but that's not what we are in this for. Dolsen's guys are ten a penny; if we lock away a dozen, he has or will find a dozen more tomorrow. Our guy is getting more and more trusted each month, and we need to see this through until we have enough on Jimmy, Davey and the rest of the inner circle, for large scale import and distribution.'

'Okay, so why pay us a visit then? Is this to warn me off Dolsen?'

'No, not really. Your super has already briefed me that you are heading up a murder investigation, arguably trumping any kind of drugs bust, but I did want to make you aware of our operation and ensure that you remain mindful of it over the course of your own. If successful, we expect Jimmy and Davey to receive twenty years inside, which is probably more than they would get for murder.'

'So, in the spirit of cooperation....bloody hell, wonders never cease.'

'It could be a benefit to your investigation, having a man on the inside.'

'But we don't have a man on the inside, we've no way of contacting him, or controlling him, passing info to him, or gathering info from him; in fact, we don't even bloody know who he is. So, no, I disagree, it isn't a benefit having a man on the inside.'

'True, and to be honest I don't expect that Dolsen's lips are that loose, you know, beyond his close family members.'

'Great. Well, of course I will remain mindful of your ongoing investigation, but unless you're in the sharing mood and can divulge a lot more that you have done so far, then you might as well have not told me. I will continue to drive forward with all lines of enquiry, and if I find the Dolsen gang at the centre of my murder, then I will take them down, without a care in the world for your drug operation.'

Priest turned to the seated Sawden. Sawden thought he was looking for his support; in actual fact Priest was expecting his support. Sawden obliged with an all too brief nod of the head in the direction of Inspector Coker.

'Right, I need to go and brief my team. Anything that you can share on what you know about the Dolsens would be helpful at this stage, inspector.'

'Funny you should say that, I have a number of my team downstairs making themselves comfortable in your incident room as we speak. Shall we, sir?'

That was the first time that Coker had verbally recognised Priest's rank or seniority, and it hadn't gone unnoticed by Priest.

'Okay, follow me. Let's get down there before World War Three starts.'

Priest and Coker arrived in the incident room, not to the sight of the respective teams squaring up to each other in an adolescent show of dominance, but Coker's four colleagues were all sitting around a table enjoying the company of the charming and ever so gorgeous PC Stacey Wright, who appeared to have each of them hanging on her every word.

'Okay, listen up, I would like to introduce Detective Inspector Coker and his team.' Priest motioned towards Coker, who accepted his cue like a seasoned stage actor.

'Sergeant Thomas, and Constables Winstanley, Woolfson and Bowen.'

'DI Coker and his colleagues are part of a team from the Serious Organised Crime Agency that has an interest in one of our suspects, Jimmy Dolsen. I think that they can provide us with some useful intel on the Dolsen family too, so I've asked DI Coker if he will provide us with a quick brief.'

Priest took his seat.

'Thank you, chief inspector. Well, I didn't arrive with a well prepared brief, I actually came to see your DCI, so let me see what I can pull out of the far recesses of the mind. Let me try and start with a bit of background and some context as to what led us here today. Operation Zeus is primarily led by SOCA, but with support from a number of CID and uniform teams across Greater Manchester. The public face of the operation has been ongoing for the last nine months, and is an extensive stop and search strategy. During this time we have stopped over nineteen hundred people, made one hundred and fourteen arrests, and seized over eighty thousand pounds of Class A drugs.'

The assembled audience appeared less than impressed with the statistics, especially the latter one.

'But, that is small potatoes compared to the bigger operation. As I said, the stop and search is the public face of the fight on street level drug distribution. The larger operation in play is targeting the mass importers and distributors. The market for illegal drugs in the UK is worth in the region of eight billion pounds each year, and rising. Just to try and put that into some tangible perspective; each year twenty tonnes of heroin, twenty-five tonnes of cocaine, and two hundred and seventy tonnes of cannabis is illegally smuggled into the UK. Our team has active operations across the North West where we estimate that an eighth of the total UK weight is distributed and consumed; that's a one billion pound illegal business that we are trying to disrupt.'

Those were the kind of figures that interested the group. 'How much of that do you, and teams like you across the UK, manage to successfully intercept?' asked Simkins, eager to learn more about an area of police work that had fascinated him for a while now.

'Well, I'm not sure on the percentages to be honest; but as an example, last year we seized two tonnes of cocaine, three quarters of a tonne of heroin, and about ten tonnes of cannabis resin. It's a good day when we, together with the Border Force, manage to prevent that kind of weight from reaching the streets, but it's just a drop in the ocean really.'

DI Coker reached down for his mug of coffee to quench his thirst and lubricate his vocal cords, although as he did he handed over to his colleague, DS Thomas. He invited him to take up the mantle from this point onwards, and Thomas duly obliged and took to his feet.

'So, aside from stories about tonnes of this and tonnes of that, what brings us here today is a potential overlap in our respective investigations. We are aware that the Dolsen family is of particular interest to your investigation, as is the network of black gangs that funnel up to its head, ultimately controlled by the Yardies. So, let me start with an introduction to the Dolsen family. I'm not sure how much of what I'm about to tell you will be useful in your own investigation, but just to know that the family are of continued interest to SOCA, should confirm that we clearly need to work collaboratively and transparently.

'My experience shows that this collaborative knowledge share, especially with you drug squad boys, is generally not bi-directional, and we end up getting royally stuffed,' piped up DS Baxter.

'Sergeant.' Priest rose to this feet, looking to further chastise his sergeant for his unnecessary remark.

DI Coker rose to his feet also. 'It's fine, sir, it's fine. Let me respond.'

Priest sat back down again.

'Sergeant…?'

'Baxter. Sergeant Baxter.'

'It is true, sergeant, that we will share some of what we know, but not all of what we know.' Coker looked up towards the wider audience. 'Quick pop quiz…anyone hazard a guess why?

As expected, DS Baxter wasn't shy in coming forward. 'Because you like shafting us and taking all the glory.' His reply received a few laughs from his seated colleagues, more for the quick riposte than the reiteration of his previous point, which had already been well made.

The experienced officers present had no interest in playing Coker's games, but the younger officers were eager to impress. DC Simkins was one of them. 'Anything to do with an informant, guv?'

'Yes, kind of. I guess that's close enough. Those of you that are aware of SOCA and have, perhaps, some experience of working alongside us, will be aware that part of our success is our ability to get undercover officers in place, and embedded within the criminal organisations that we target. It's an extremely high risk strategy, and one that can place our officers in significant danger every day. However, the benefits can be…well, the benefits are obvious and speak for themselves. In this instance, we do have an undercover officer within the Dolsen gang, and that is pretty much all that I can, or want to, divulge at this point in time. I have had earlier conversations with your super and DCI and reassured them, as I do you now, that we will do all we can to support the information and intelligence gathering to assist in your murder investigations should the Dolsen family be involved, but we won't compromise either our officer, or our own ongoing operation.'

'Like I said, one way,' muttered Baxter, just audible enough for those immediately around him to hear.

'Let me start by sharing some intel on the Dolsen family,' DS Thomas began, 'the Dolsens are a traditional, old school, white family gang. Think back to the Krays of the sixties, wind forward fifty years and you're there; just substitute protection rackets for drug distribution. They have no real ambition or power to expand much beyond Greater Manchester. They are, however, one of the more dominant gangs that control a large part of the drug supply in an area that stretches from the M6 across to Stalybridge, north up to Accrington and Blackburn, and down as far as Macclesfield. We reckon that there are twelve other gangs in Manchester, all organised and serious players that are subservient to the Dolsens. Some of whom will be at their beck and call, whereas others will…sub-contract…for want of a better word, when the Dolsens want something doing. But, these other gangs will still have their own activities going on.'

'Who are the key players then, sarge?'

'The family is headed by James Dolsen, known as Jimmy to most people. Thirty-eight years old, he has been the brawn and brains of the family since he started petty crime in his early teenage years. He started with an early spate of burglary, before progressing to street muggings and eventually into drugs. If you ever get to his house, check out his pride and joy sitting on the drive, his 1973 Jensen Interceptor. It's a bit of a shit tip if you ask me and clearly next to worthless these days, but it is rumoured that he bought it for cash with the first twenty grand that he earned selling ecstasy during the Manchester rave scene in the eighties.'

DS Thomas could see the puzzled look on some of the younger officers' faces, thinking *WTF is a Jensen Interceptor? Sounds like something from one of the Mad Max movies.*

'Jimmy Dolsen has three siblings. His right-hand man is his brother Davey. Davey appears to be the doer, the enforcer of the family. If something needs doing, Davey is your man, whatever it is. He has a reputation of being a nasty, hard bastard, and unfortunately his reputation has been well earned. He has done two stretches in prison, both for aggravated assault; the first time he served eighteen months, and the second thirty-two months. Wherever you find Davey, trouble won't be too far behind.'

'What about the bird that was killed then, sarge?'

DC Simkins received the expected moans, groans, heckles and projectile pens for the less than diplomatic and sexist question. The SOCA sergeant knew all too well whom he was referring to.

'The dead woman from last night was his sister, Victoria. Victoria and her twin Shaun, thirty-two, make up the remaining siblings. As far as we can ascertain, Victoria was never really involved in any illegal activities, but she certainly traded off the family name. She was a regular on the high-end club scene in Manchester, and she certainly made sure that everyone knew that she was a Dolsen. In the main, that just meant that she was guaranteed entry into clubs, didn't have to wait outside in queues, secured tables in exclusive VIP areas, and probably quaffed hundreds of bottles of complimentary champagne.'

'And her twin, Shaun?'

'Shaun is an up and coming member of the family gang, gaining more prominence with each passing month, we hear. We are reliably informed that Shaun has recently been entrusted with the running of their pub and club business. Now, this is predominately legitimate, as you would expect it to be. Jimmy Dolsen owns three night-clubs and at least eight pubs that we can see across the North West. They all have the necessary licences across health and safety, fire regulations, music and alcohol, and they themselves turn over a tidy sum. However, aligned to their core interests, there is a high volume of drugs that are moved in these premises, especially the nightclubs. There is only one dealer allowed in these places; part of Dolsen's crew obviously. The dealer is protected by the door staff or security team on site, and any independent dealers are dealt with severely.'

'Severely?' DC Simkins was positively salivating at the storyline and desperate for more gruesome details.

'Yes, there were two instances, separated across two different nightclubs, and by about fifteen months. Two individuals who were either too dumb to realise it was a Dolsen-owned club, or who actually knew and were even dumber to believe they could peddle their shit independently in the club. We came across both of them after they had been admitted to hospital; one had two broken arms and a couple of broken ribs. The other got away lightly, although his face looked like it had been in the ring with Mike Tyson for the better part of a dozen rounds. Neither of them provided anything useful for any charges to be brought.'

The sergeant paused to take a gulp of his coffee which was now stone cold, and he spat it back into the mug.

'The final name you need to know is Christopher. Christopher Dolsen is cousin to the siblings, and has always been regarded as a close member of the family. His role, would you believe it – get this for a white family gang in the North West of England – is intelligence. Apparently, Christopher is so well connected to Manchester's network of loan sharks, fraudsters, rogue landlords, counterfeiters and general all round horrible scumbags, it is rumoured that he gets to know everything that is going down, before it happens. A bloody great position to be in, if you are one of the dominant crime families in the North West.'

DI Coker rose to his feet and thanked his sergeant.

'Well, that's the runners and riders in the Dolsen family. Before we bring you up to speed with the Yardies, let me share with you some of the facts and figures that reinforce why this gang is considered to be a major player, and why I guarantee that they would use any and all force to protect their business interests; and that includes the brutal murder of their competition. We estimate that the Dolsen family will distribute one hundred and fifty kilos of coke, three hundred kilos of weed, and up to five hundred thousand ecstasy tabs this year. They also distribute heroin and amphetamines, but our estimates on volumes there are more guesswork. We reckon that this pulls in almost eleven million pounds for the family.'

'Eleven million, really?' came a voice from the audience.

'Best estimates, based on weight and street values, yes.'

'Where the hell do they spend it, or hide it...or... whatever they do with it?'

'That is currently the million dollar question, or the eleven million pound question. Finding out where the money ends up is clearly one of our two major objectives within our operation. We would hope to follow the money trail and apply the appropriate leverage to tie the Dolsens directly to the money.'

'And what is your other major objective?' asked Priest.

'The second one, whilst less likely, is to catch Jimmy and Davey directly handling a significant shipment. Sizeable enough to put them away for twenty to twenty-five years. From there, the infrastructure of the gang is likely to start crumbling, especially as other gangs will become bolder and more aggressive, muscling in on the weight that the Dolsens would have normally controlled.'

'Isn't that just moving the problem from one gang to another?'

'Yes, kind of. Although I have said that other gangs will pick up the natural supply and demand, the Dolsens have built their illegal empire over the last twenty years, and I anticipate it would take another ten, perhaps seven years if they're lucky, for anyone else to make the same waves that Jimmy has done. As they take on more weight, and perhaps move into geographical areas that they are not familiar with, they take higher risks and the chances of us being able to pin something on them, something substantial that sticks, weighs high in our favour.'

'Makes sense, guv. Makes sense,' Simkins was quick to agree.

'Indeed it does. We don't just make this shit up, you know.' Coker's statement was followed by a jocular smile to all.

'One of the elements that has made the Dolsens so successful over the last two decades is that their business ethos appears to be more entrepreneurial rather than territorial. From the door staff on their pubs and clubs, to the hundred or so street dealers, to the network of contacts known to the family through Christopher, Jimmy is known to foster and support an inclusive entrepreneurial spirit. It's easy to recruit soldiers, most of whom already have no employment prospects and a deep seated hatred for the police; it's easy for everyone to make loads of money, and if you show particular aptitude, it's relatively easy to get your face known within the Dolsen hierarchy. Having said that, and irrespective of initiative, Jimmy Dolsen is known to rule his empire with the metaphorical iron fist.'

The assembled crowd were clearly hanging on his every word, engrossed by tales of violent drug gangs and the trappings of their wealth. Most of them had temporarily forgotten about the reason that SOCA were actually there.

'Let me finish on the Dolsens with a couple of facts, one of which will simply blow your mind, and the second of which may be pertinent to your investigation, either now or in the not too distant future. Firstly, you'll remember that I said the annual income from drugs is worth about eleven million to the Dolsen family; well it is estimated that their impact to the economy across the North West of England is one billion pounds.'

'Fuck me!' Simkins was astounded. No more so than anyone else, he just appeared to verbalise his astonishment loudly.

'Exactly.'

'That's bollocks; how did you get to that figure? That's just a made up number, finger in the air type shit.' DS Baxter had rejoined the conversation.

'Okay, let me take a brief minute,' Coker looked at Priest, aware that he was digressing, and had been for some time, 'a very brief minute.'

Priest smiled at him diplomatically and courteously.

'If you consider that the Dolsens are involved, to a certain degree, in everything from money spent on drugs that should be spent legally in the general economy; or property tenancies where the rental payments are not declared; or the counterfeit goods where the revenues are taken from the pockets of manufacturers and retailers. Factor in the labour, or gang members, that should have jobs and contribute to society in terms of taxes. Then you can go to the nth degree by factoring in the cost to the National

Health Service by all those involved in the gang activities, that don't directly contribute towards the social system, but draw upon it when necessary. To be honest, guys, half a dozen brain cells in a room with a calculator for a couple of hours, and you can easily see how this particular gang does have a negative impact, directly and indirectly, on the local economy of up to one billion pounds.'

'And the second fact. The one more pertinent to our investigation?' invited Priest.

'Yes, sorry... The Dolsens do appear to have a weapon of choice. It might not be relevant now, but is worth noting that they tend to favour the 9mm Baikal 12H-79 hand-gun. We believe that they buy them from a Lithuanian gang, who in turn smuggle these handguns all the way from Russia. They pay top dollar for them, anywhere up to nine hundred per handgun. Our guy on the inside has seen many members strapped with these guns.'

'Thank you, DI Coker.' Priest stepped forward. 'Let's stretch our legs and refill our coffee for ten or fifteen minutes.' Priest looked at his watch. 'Back here at quarter past please.'

'Too much info, or just right?' Coker enquired.

'Background info on the Dolsens is great, thank you. If we can tie this up with some comparable background info on the Yardies, then I think it gives us a good solid foundation of understanding as we take our investigation forward.'

'Guv, can I borrow you?' DS Stephens interjected.

'Sure.' They walked over towards Priest's office, entered and closed the door.

'What do you think, Nic, is this info from Coker and his team helpful?'

'Not sure if it will be ultimately helpful in our murder investigations, but the background detail on the Dolsens and the Yardies should help us understand that culture better, and perhaps why there has suddenly started what appears to be a murderous tit-for-tat. And perhaps more importantly, it might help us to understand the players, and who ordered the murders, if not carried them out themselves.'

'Good, I agree. I'll give the SOCA boys another half an hour on the Yardies, then I'll kick them out and we can get back to our current lines of enquiry. So, what did you want?'

'I took a call from the pathology lab about ten minutes ago, Doctor Bell has rushed through the autopsy on Victoria Dolsen.'

'Okay, what does it tell us that we don't already know?'

Stephens smiled, 'nothing to be honest. Our victim was shot seventeen times and would have certainly died from massive blood loss, but one of the bullets punctured her heart, and this, the doctor has given as the cause of death.'

'Seventeen bullets, did you say?'

'Yes.'

'Bloody mad, Nic.'

'I know; poor girl; especially if she was an innocent victim.'

'Hmmm, I'm going to reserve judgement on her involvement, or at least, her awareness or ignorance as to what her family was involved in.'

'Bit harsh,' noted Stephens, 'but okay.'

'Okay, thanks, Nic. No surprises from the doctor then. I'll announce the findings to the team after SOCA have gone.'

Priest and Stephens engaged in further discussion, mainly around what they should cook for dinner tonight. As they vacated the office, the team had returned to their seats and were waiting on the second instalment of SOCA's briefing.

'Right, are we ready to continue?' Priest looked in DI Coker's direction, who provided a nod in return. 'Okay, DI Coker is going to provide some background on the second of the drug gangs that are likely to be involved in our double murder investigation; the all too infamous Yardies. Inspector…'

'Thank you. I understand that you were all briefed recently by Charles Mayfield. Mr Mayfield is a contractor who works with several units within the police force, including SOCA. I'm sure Mr Mayfield provided you with plenty of background on the culture, organisation and impact that the Yardies have across the North West, if not the UK as a whole. We just want to fill in some gaps about their drug operation.'

When DI Coker said 'we' he clearly meant the royal 'we' and he took his seat, whereupon DS Thomas took to his feet again.

'The Yardies control the supply of crack cocaine in the North West. Our experience shows that they tend not to handle other forms of illegal drugs, and in the main, other gangs appear to have little interest in muscling in on the crack market, which is probably why they never really have disputes with other gangs. Their operation in the North West is big, and I mean fucking huge. We estimate that they will control up to two thousand kilos this year, and their business continues to grow year on year. Their operation will net them around forty million pounds this year.

91

The main man was Jarel Powell, the guy that you found dead recently. We estimate that he had a personal fortune of fifty million pounds, although this itself is almost impossible to verify.'

The room echoed with synchronous utterings of *fifty million quid.*

'As Mr Mayfield no doubt explained, there are twenty to thirty main soldiers in the gang, those involved in the operations and who pose a significant firearms threat in support of the operation. On the periphery, there are probably another one hundred and fifty; these are the soldiers that handle the distribution and street level dealing. Finally, the weapon of choice for these morons is the MAC-10 automatic submachine gun. Affectionately known as the spray and pray weapon, firing twelve hundred rounds a minute, you can probably see why. However, it's actually very rare to be honest, to have been involved in, or to have heard about any serious gun battles, or any spray and pray style shootings involving the Yardies. There are three main reasons for this; firstly as I mentioned earlier, the lack of direct competitors lends itself to a relatively stable and untroubled existence. Secondly, and as Mr Mayfield will have mentioned, lots of their dirty work is carried out by some of the subservient black gangs in the area, thus allowing the Yardies to maintain clean hands. And finally, well, the Yardies have done an incredible job over the last two or three decades projecting themselves as the meanest motherfuckers in town, that no-one would dare fuck with, thus reinforcing this perpetual circle of; perception and image leading to intimidation, intimidation in turn feeding the perception and image.'

DS Thomas nodded towards Coker and took his seat.

'Thank you, sergeant. Let me just wrap up with some general info. Some of you will no doubt be aware that the multi-agency Integrated Gang Management Unit established over ten years ago now has had a significant impact on the gangs across the North West of England. Gang related shootings fell by almost ninety percent in the following years. Manchester especially is not the Wild West that it might once have been, and thankfully shootings are a rare occurrence these days. The last gang related gun fatality was in Moss Side some seven years ago. Don't get me wrong, there have been dozens of shootings since, but none directly attributable or proven to be disputes between drug gangs. That being said, these latest shootings, in fact the two murders that you are investigating are cause for concern, especially as there is a high probability that this will escalate further. Personally I don't see Victoria Dolsen being the last victim that you will mop up off the streets of Manchester in the next few weeks.'

After seeing Coker and his team out of the station, Priest was back in his office, packing up his briefcase and about to head out for the night when DC Simkins appeared in his doorframe.

'Robert, what can I do for you?'

'I've got an update on Johannes, guv.'

'Who?'

'Johannes De Groot, you know, the boyfriend.' At which point, DS Stephens came up behind Simkins and pushed him forward into Priest's office.

'Come on, Robert, if you're in, you're in.'

'Shit, sorry, Robert, I had forgotten all about him.'

'About who?' Stephens enquired.

'Victoria Dolsen's boyfriend,' confirmed Simkins.

'Ah, Johannes De Groot,' confidently recalled Stephens.

'Alright, smart arse. Sorry, Robert, yes, how is he getting on?'

'I've just come off the phone from the hospital; I managed to speak to the lead consultant that operated on him early this morning. Bless him, he was still on duty, I swear he must have worked a twelve-hour day so far, and he said he had much more to do before he knocked off.'

Priest displayed a dreary, lacklustre and ponderous face that sometimes manifested itself when he was bored, and waiting for the conversation to gain some momentum, asked, 'and?'

'Oh yes, sorry, guv. Well, miraculously Mr De Groot survived surgery. He had seven bullets removed during a successful five-hour operation.'

'Wow, that's bloody great,' acknowledged Priest.

'He's currently in intensive care, and to be honest, guv, I was advised that it's touch and go as to whether he'll survive or not.'

'Okay, so we shouldn't bank on being able to interview him any time soon?'

'Guv, we shouldn't bank on interviewing him at all. If he wakes, it will be a miracle, and if, just if, he is able to recall anything useful, well that will be…' Simkins paused, 'what's better than a miracle?'

'A revelation, Robert,' Stephens helped him out, 'probably a revelation, or a phenomenon.' Neither of the words really suited the context, but then he had chosen 'miracle' and in reality, by very definition you would be hard pushed to beat a miracle.

'Okay. Can you check in with the hospital, perhaps every two or three days, and keep us all updated on his progress, and importantly, when he is conscious?'

'Yes, guv, of course.' DC Simkins moved to exit the room, but only got as far as the door.

'Robert.'

'Yes, guv.'

'CCTV. I forgot to ask. What did we turn up from any CCTV?'

'Nothing, guv. There were only two shops with cameras, both of which were dummies, and the traffic cameras, well you wouldn't bloody believe it if I told you.'

There then followed an uncomfortable silence, broken by a somewhat perplexed Priest. 'Well? I am asking you to tell me.'

'Oh yes, sorry. Well, the two street cameras that would probably have caught the incident needed to be rebooted due to a persistent fault. Apparently they were offline between four-fifteen and four twenty-five.'

'And let me guess…'

'Yes, guv, footage prior to the reboot doesn't show anyone there, and footage after the reboot shows the couple already on the ground. The camera picked up a taxi, and this was confirmed as Mohammed Akthar, the taxi driver that made the 999 call around four-thirty. We spoke to him on the morning.'

'Yes, I recall. Okay, thanks, Robert, and like I said earlier, keep me updated on the boyfriend's progress.'

'Yes, guv.' Simkins left the room.

'You're not hanging your hopes on the boyfriend are you, Jonny?'

'Me? No.'

'Good, because, as sad as it is, I personally don't think he'll survive.'

'No, perhaps not.'

'And if he does…well I don't know, but I would be surprised if he remembered anything that would be useful to us.'

'Yes, sadly I agree, Nic, on both parts. Anyway, investigation aside, I hope he pulls through.'

'Me too.'

CHAPTER 8

The pavement was being pounded with an unseasonable torrent of rain as a black Range Rover pulled up. Simon Darby, one of the two doormen, stepped out from underneath the canopy that had been keeping him dry, and towards the driver's door.

'Evening, Shaun.'

'Simon. Glad you're on tonight. How are you?' He threw Simon the keys to the car.

'Good thanks, Shaun. I'll move your motor around the back.'

'Nah, get some fucker else to do it.' He looked in the direction of the other doorman standing under the canopy that covered the entrance to the club, 'Tony will do it; 'ere, Tony, park the motor for me, pal.'

Tony stepped forward and took the keys from Simon. Despite being less amiable than Simon regarding the menial tasks sometimes thrown at them by Jimmy, Davey or Shaun, Tony knew it wasn't worth going to battle for, and needed to keep his job. So he bit his lip and carried out the tasks with a perfunctory acknowledgement.

'How we doing then, Simon? Is the club busy tonight? Business good?' Shaun wasn't interested in how many clubbers were drinking and spending their money in the club, one of the many clubs owned by the Dolsen family. The Adelphi was a front for their drug business, in fact it was one of many fronts. The club was an opportunity not only to deal drugs to the punters, but on a much larger scale, it provided an opportunity to launder millions of pounds of drug money. Intelligent and well thought through scams, such as periodical free entry to the public, but the books showed five hundred people having paid fifteen pounds entry fee; to private parties where punters paid thousands to have exclusive access to the club, on a standard Saturday night open to the public, through to the obvious and large scale scams on purchase and consumption of alcohol volume that simply didn't exist. On a typical Saturday night, the club probably legitimately averaged around thirty-five thousand pounds in alcohol sales, but the books always showed that the high-rollers were in town, with average sales of fifty, sometimes sixty or seventy thousand pounds in a single night. The average spend per punter per visit of one hundred and forty pounds wasn't unreasonable when the phantom volume of champagne quaffed was taken into account.

'Bit quiet tonight, Shaun, well so far it is. Plenty to move tonight, but it's still early.'

'That's the attitude, Simon, that's the attitude we need. Right, I'm off in, I'll catch you later.'

'Okay, Shaun.'

As Shaun reached the roped off VIP area, Davey and Christopher were already sitting there, each with a voluptuous, half naked woman draped over them, nibbling on their ears, whispering whatever the boys wanted to hear, and generally hanging on their every word, in between draining bottomless glasses of champagne. The boys were loving it.

'Take a break, ladies, go get a drink,' said Shaun as he dropped his arse onto the luxurious black leather chesterfield settee.

'Oi.' Davey wasn't used to being told what to do by his younger sibling.

'You'll have time for the birds later, Davey. We need to talk.' Christopher offered him a glass of champagne as he sat down.

'I don't want any of that shit.' He reached out to one of the VIP hostesses who was within earshot, saying, 'get me a double Jack Daniels and coke please.'

'Of course, Shaun.' The VIP waitress was positively fawning all over him. Her three words, whispered in a smoky sultry voice, might as well have been *come fuck me*.

Shaun waited until the waitress had brought his drink, then dismissed her in a brazen and arrogant manner that left her sauntering away licking her wounds, and unsure what she had said or done to upset him. Shaun wasn't one to upset if she wanted to keep her job.

'We need to decide on our response; we need to decide how many of those fuckers are going to pay for Victoria.'

'Fucking twenty of the bastards, and right now. Let's gather the lads and pay them a visit tonight,' said Christopher. 'We can take twenty of the fuckers in one go,' he added.

'I'm with you on the desire,' said Davey, 'but it's not going to be tonight. This shit takes time to organise, days if not weeks of recon work, as you know.'

'Does it?' questioned Shaun, 'what's stopping us from taking a dozen lads, all tooled up, to find the Yardie scum tonight?'

'Planning, Shaun, and the risk that we don't know what we will be walking into. The risk that we will take a dozen men, run into an army, and lose most of the lads. Including fucking me.'

'So what? We are avenging Victoria. It will take what it takes until all of those fuckers are dead.'

'Agreed in principle, but we need to minimise further losses on our side, Shaun. We've got guys that have been loyal to us for years, and we can't just throw a dozen of them into the lion's den, so that we can take out a like number of the Yardie scum.'

'So you propose that we do fuck all then?'

'No, that's not what I'm saying. We plan, and we avenge, but we include Jimmy, and Jimmy will want to plan every detail to ensure that we mitigate any risks, and that we all walk away unscathed from any attack.'

'It'll be too late by then, the message will be lost, forgotten, we need to hammer home the message, and do it now.'

'What message? Don't be fucking stupid; today, tomorrow, next month, next year, we will avenge Victoria and the outcome will be the same…complete fucking annihilation for those Yardie bastards. We'll wipe out an entire fucking generation, trust me.'

Two hours, four bottles of champagne, six beers and five JD and cokes later, the trio had taken a significant step towards the when, where, who and how, as Jimmy came into sight.

Davey started to say something to Jimmy, but his slurred speech made his words totally incomprehensible.

'How much has he had to drink?' Jimmy pointed at Davey and directed his question to the other two.

'Same as us, Jimmy.'

'Too fucking much then. I can't understand a word, Davey.'

Davey sat forward and composed himself. 'Understand this; we are planning to exact revenge for Victoria. We are going to take down the entire North West fucking Yardies.'

'Really, Davey? You and whose army?'

'Army? My fucking army.'

'Oh, you have an army, do you? Where is your army? And it's yours to command, is it?'

'Yes, well...no, well it's our fucking army, Jimmy, ours.'

Jimmy sat forward in his seat and beckoned the other three to do likewise. 'Listen, firstly nobody is killing anybody. We will not be going to war with the Yardies, is that clear? Secondly, if we had an army, and we fucking don't, it would be me who decides when and how it is deployed.'

'So you're just going to let them get away with it then?'

'No, Davey, I'm not, but you pick your battles and the timing of them; and I'm telling you that right now isn't the right time for this, for revenge.'

'Fucking pussy,' came the swift retort from Davey. Jimmy chose not to respond, but to rise from his chair and walk away out of the VIP area and into the bustling crowd.

Two black BMW X6 vehicles had been driving two hundred metres apart in almost fluid synchronicity for the last three hours, and were almost at their destination. The drive from Southampton had been quiet and uneventful, exactly as they would have wanted it. In between the two BMW's was an unassuming silver Vauxhall Vectra. The three cars had been driving in a convoy for the last one hundred and eighty miles, and were now on the outskirts of Nottingham city centre.

If you knew what you were looking for, and with the benefit of hindsight, it would be clear that the two BMW's were providing protection for the Vauxhall. One in front and one behind, but never too close for it to be obvious that the convoy was three cars. If you passed them on the motorway, it simply looked like the family saloon car had overtaken one of the BMW's and had settled back into his position on the road, and that whilst it could easily have been assumed that the two BMW X6 were 'together', their distance from each other dispelled most thoughts of any organised close quarter protection.

Should either of the BMW's be pulled over by the police, the Vauxhall would simply peel off at the first available opportunity, clearly signalling that it wasn't with those two vehicles, and just happened to find itself in a BMW sandwich for a period of time. It was highly unlikely given the choice that the police would look to stop the family saloon car as opposed to the big, meaty BMW's with blacked-out windows. It was arguable that the two escort vehicles could, and should, have been more understated family saloons themselves; although this was never close to being a winning argument with the occupants. Either way, BMW SUV's were ten a penny on the roads these days, and no more likely to be pulled over by traffic police than a sales rep in his Toyota.

The first BMW pulled up at the side of the road, outside a disused and dilapidated building. The warehouse was one of a number of buildings on the Belvedere South Industrial Estate in the southwest of the city, located adjacent to the River Trent. Companies had long since vacated the fifties-built industrial estate in favour of the more modern enterprise areas to the east of the city centre.

The Belvedere South Industrial Estate hadn't undergone any redevelopment as yet, and largely stood untouched from the point at which the last company had moved out, about seven years ago.

The BMW needed to wait no longer than thirty seconds before a figure appeared out of the darkness and moved to open the closed gates at the entrance to the warehouse. By this time, the first car had been joined by the other two, and they all drove in and towards the roller shutters that were opening for them as they approached. As they entered the inside of the warehouse, the two BMW's peeled off left and right respectively and allowed the Vauxhall to continue forward towards the centre of the warehouse where a collection of other cars were waiting.

The inside of the warehouse was relatively clear; anything left by the previous occupants, even of doubtful value, had long been stripped out and taken by opportunistic thieves targeting abandoned warehouses. There was no artificial lighting inside, the electricity having been disconnected a long time ago, but the warehouse did benefit from half a dozen large windows on the rear wall. Despite the build-up of general dirt, grime and pigeon excrement over time, the windows were still effective at letting through lots of natural light; and with tonight being a full moon in a cloudless sky, the inside of the warehouse was illuminated sufficiently for everyone to see, and do, what was necessary.

The first occupants to alight were from the BMW's. Each vehicle had three occupants and they made their way towards the Vauxhall some fifteen metres in front of where they had parked. At the same time, the driver and sole occupant of the Vauxhall opened the door and stepped out. The female, about mid-thirties in age and of Caribbean origin, left the driver's door open and started to walk back towards the BMW's. Her job was done, her job was clear – drive the vehicle from Southampton to Nottingham, be aware of the escorting cars but don't acknowledge them, take the appropriate and pre-agreed evasive action should the police intercept one or both of the escorting vehicles. And if she herself was pulled by the police, keep her mouth shut and hope to God that they didn't open the boot.

She received a brief acknowledgement from one of the others as she walked past, then simply entered the rear door of the BMW, closed it, and wasn't to be seen again.

The other group whom they had come to meet had arrived an hour earlier, and with a similar approach. They were already standing outside of their vehicles, two luxurious Mercedes GLE-AMG and a rather smart Mercedes A-class hatchback.

Two of the men from the Mercedes group approached the Vauxhall.

'Wi cool?'

'Yeh, wi cool, mon.'

'No nize?'

'Nutten; a smood ride, mon. Every ting irie.'

'Okay, let dam see wot wi av ere.'

One of the men opened the boot of the Vauxhall to reveal twenty-five neatly wrapped, perfectly formed packages. Crack cocaine. Twenty-five bricks with a street value of one and a quarter million pounds.

The buyers didn't need to check the merchandise; these two Yardie gangs had been doing business for many a year, and the merchandise had always proven to be top quality.

Two of the buyers set about carrying the twenty-five bricks from the Vauxhall to their Mercedes, whilst two others proceeded to exchange handshakes, fist bumps and a couple of marijuana joints in the time it took to transfer them. One of the buyers returned from the last leg of the transfer with a small black leather holdall, which he duly handed to one of the others.

The holdall was passed to the sellers, then passed back to another and taken to their vehicle. The bag contained cash; used notes, and lots of them; but the contents were not checked, and the cash was not counted. The trust was mutual for both the drugs and the cash. Both parties had been doing regular business for many years, and whilst both gangs had deep-seated Yardie roots, that would have counted for nothing if one had decided to cheat, steal from or double-cross the other.

The buyers sped out of the warehouse in a tight convoy, and once of out of the industrial estate and onto the main arterial road, would follow the same cautious approach and protocols on their way back to Manchester.

CHAPTER 9

P riest had had eyes on Shaun Dolsen since the shift started at eight a.m. although there had been nothing of any substance to report so far. His radio crackled into life.

'Guv, Shaun Dolsen has just left his house with another guy. Both occupants are in Dolsen's Range Rover, and are currently heading down Byford Road. Do you want me to maintain eyes on them?'

'Affirmative. Stay with them, but make sure that you're not seen. I'm leaving the station now, so dependent on what route they take, I should be in position to intercept in about fifteen minutes or so.'

'Roger, out.'

DS Stephens started to laugh.

Priest smiled at her. 'What's funny? What are you laughing at?'

'Peter makes me laugh. I've never heard anyone be so formal on the radio...roger, out...proper old school, is Sergeant Grainger,' she chuckled to herself again. 'Then again, you're just as bad with your...affirmative.'

'How quickly you forget what you're taught at the academy, and what correct radio protocol sounds like.'

'Not really, Jonny, I haven't forgotten, and I'm sure most coppers haven't. It's just too old school and people don't use it anymore, people don't talk that way anymore. We say 'yes' not 'affirmative', and we say 'okay' as opposed to 'roger and out'.'

'I guess so,' conceded Priest, 'I'll try and be more modern and relevant, Nic. How does that sound?'

'Just be yourself, Jonny,' replied Stephens, 'but, perhaps, maybe remove that formality stick from up your arse.'

'Formality stick?'

'Formality stick, Jonny.'

It took Priest and Stephens just over ten minutes to be within a couple of hundred metres of Dolsen's Range Rover. Grainger had been providing a running commentary, and had ensured that they stayed en-route to intercept.

Grainger recognised the unmarked CID car behind him, and pulled in to his left to let Priest pass. Priest was now two cars behind Dolsen, which was where he stayed for almost two miles. He wasn't expecting any trouble when he eventually pulled Dolsen over, but he could never be sure; this gang were serious players in the North West drug trafficking market, and as the last couple of weeks had proven, they would probably do just about anything to protect their business and themselves. And that might just include shooting a police officer in broad daylight.

Despite the risks, Priest waited until Dolsen was on a stretch of dual carriageway heading out of the city centre, and with no residential area within sight, he made a swift and decisive move to overtake the vehicle in front and pull in immediately behind Dolsen. With the covert 'blues' flashing, the car ahead signalled its intent to pull over to the side. There was a lay-by approaching some one hundred metres ahead, so Dolsen bided his time and pulled into the lay-by, as would any sensible driver not wanting to pull up at the side of a fast, busy road. Once stationary, he could be seen unbuckling his seatbelt but remained seated.

'Am I coming too?' asked Stephens.

'Do you want to?'

'Errrrr, yes. What did you think? I'm not sitting in the bloody car waiting for you like a rookie probationer.'

'Okay, come on then. You approach the passenger side, and just be on your guard. I'm not expecting anything to kick off, but I can't be sure.'

'Firearms?'

'Yes, possibly, Nic.'

'Then, shouldn't we…'

'No, like I said, I'm really not expecting any adverse reaction from Dolsen. Do you want to wait in the car?'

'No.'

'Okay then, let's go.'

They both exited the car and started to walk towards the front doors of the Range Rover, the chunky wing mirrors clearly reflecting that both the driver and the passenger were watching them as they approached.

Dolsen leant forward and reached under the car seat with an outstretched right arm, and his passenger knew immediately what he was reaching for. 'Don't be fucking daft, Shaun, leave it. We're going to be in enough fucking trouble if they search the motor and find it.'

Dolsen retracted his arm and sat back just as Priest reached his window. Priest gestured for him to wind down his window, but Dolsen took the opportunity to wind him up with a like-minded hand and finger gesture, and a crass attempt at mocking sign language. Dolsen turned to his passenger and they both started laughing. Priest was unamused; he tapped on the window and again gestured with his finger for the window to be wound down. Once again, Dolsen started to howl with laughter, and only when his laughter had abated did he press the button that wound down the window.

'Sorry, officer, I didn't know what you wanted. You were throwing your finger around in all sorts of shapes and patterns; I thought you were doing a finger dance for me.'

'A finger dance?'

'Yes.' Dolsen started to copy what Priest had been doing, but with extreme exaggeration and a lot of artistic licence.

'You're an idiot, Dolsen.' That got his attention; that had stopped him in his tracks. The one thing that really annoyed Shaun Dolsen was being told he was 'stupid' or 'thick' or that he was 'an idiot'. His father took great delight during his childhood in constantly berating him and knocking his confidence. He was always 'a disappointment' and 'would never amount to much in life'. Shaun wouldn't have minded so much if that was just his dad's way, and if he treated Jimmy, Davey or even his twin sister Victoria in a similar way, but he didn't. For reasons that had never been clear, his dad appeared to single out Shaun as the runt of the family. As Shaun grew older, into his early twenties, he had wished many times that his father was still alive; initially so he could give him a bloody good beating, but as he aged and mellowed a little, it was more to show his father that he had made something of his life – he had a nice house, an expensive car, a brace of brand new Rolex watches, and a wealth of other material 'trinkets'. Although he was under no illusions that his father would still have found fault with him; if his father ever became aware of how he actually earned his money – and the shit would have definitely hit the fan then – he would have absolutely honed in on the materialistic element of Shaun's success. 'Success? Pfffft,' Shaun could hear his voice, 'all you've done is buy stuff; having a car and an overpriced wristwatch doesn't make you successful, Shaun, it simply demonstrates that you can't manage money and that you waste it at every opportunity.' Yes, actually Shaun was glad his father was no longer alive.

Priest looked beyond Dolsen towards the passenger. 'And you are?'

'Me? Nobody.'

'Name?'

'Name? You don't know your own name? Look at your warrant card, officer, that'll probably shed some light on it.' Priest was less than amused.

'Name,' he repeated, this time with a much firmer tone.

After a brief pause, 'Darby, Simon Darby,' came the response.

'Where are we off to, Dolsen?'

'We, officer? I'm not sure that 'we' are going anywhere, are we?' He grossly exaggerated the last word. Priest rose to a perfunctory smile, but didn't bite further.

'Anyway, why have you pulled me over?'

'I wanted a chat.'

'A chat?'

'Yes, a chat. You know, with the infamous Shaun Dolsen.'

'Infamous? I think you've got the wrong guy, occi-fer.' His childish mispronunciation of the word drew forced laughter from both occupants. 'Anyway, as fucking mind-bendingly enthralling as that would probably be, you need just cause to stop and search.'

'Stop and search? Nobody said anything about searching you, or the car.' Priest looked over at the passenger who simply rolled his eyes and turned his head away, although immediately in the face of DS Stephens, he turned it back again. There was something about the passenger, but Priest couldn't put his finger on it.

'Well, like I said, where is your just cause, or probable cause, or whatever the fuck it's called?'

'You've been watching too many US cop dramas, Dolsen. It's simply called stop and search. I hadn't thought about searching you, or the vehicle for that matter, but do you know what…I might just do that now.' He looked up over the roof towards Stephens. 'What do you reckon, sergeant, credible evidence received informing us that this vehicle is likely to be concealing illegal drugs, or a weapon, or both perhaps?'

It was a rhetorical question, and DS Stephens simply provided an acknowledging shrug of her shoulders.

'Go on then, get on with it. I haven't got all fucking day.' Dolsen's cocky demeanour was starting to cause concern for his passenger; his thoughts were clearly on the handgun that was stashed under the driver's seat, and its potential discovery that could land them both in prison for a minimum term of five years. This perhaps wasn't a time for Shaun to be cocky.

As Dolsen and Priest went eye to eye for the briefest of moments, his bluff paid off as Priest stood up straight and smiled. 'I'm watching you, Shaun; you and your family, all of your family.'

The passenger, who had been relatively quiet and inactive in the discussion to this point aside from having to confirm his name, turned to Stephens and visually checked her up and down in a blatant sexual manner as he hung his head out of the window towards her.

'You don't say much, do you, sweetheart? How about you and me hit the town tonight? Give me your address and I'll pick you up; shall we say about eight?'

'You can say what you want,' replied Stephens, 'I don't date drug dealers.'

'Labels, labels…I hate being labelled. I mean *drug dealer,* it's such a harsh and abrasive, let alone untrue, label.' He pulled himself up out of his seat, his head and upper body leaning further out of the window. Stephens didn't recoil, but stood her ground as he was almost eye to eye.

'On second thoughts, you're fucking ugly and I've got a reputation for not shagging fucking ugly birds; especially those that look like a bulldog chewing a wasp.' He slid back down into his seat and turned to Dolsen. They both started laughing.

Priest caught Stephens' eye and tipped his head in a gesture she understood. They both stood upright and started to walk back to their vehicle. Dolsen leaned out of his door window, facing towards the departing officers.

'Oi,' no reply, 'oi,' no reply, 'have a good day, occifer.'

Dolsen put the car in gear and sped off before Priest and Stephens had settled back into their car.

An inexperienced police officer might at this point have turned to Priest questioning what the point of the last ten minutes was, but DS Stephens knew the charade was designed simply to wind up Dolsen. Although the jury was out as to whether it had worked or not.

After an hour back at the station, it finally clicked for Priest. He knew that the passenger in Dolsen's car looked familiar to him, but hadn't been able to place him until now. In fact, he still didn't know exactly who he was, but he had a pretty good idea of where to start asking questions. A quick phone call and a meeting was arranged for later that afternoon.

Priest had decided to attend on his own, and walked into the Crown and Anchor pub a full ten minutes before the scheduled meeting time. Upon his arrival he observed that the guy he was due to meet was also dutifully prompt, sitting at a table, but without a drink. After managing to make eye contact, and performing the universally accepted hand gesture for *do you want a drink?* Priest settled down at the table across from Detective Inspector Coker.

'As I said on the phone, earlier this morning we pulled Shaun Dolsen. Not for anything specific, it was just a road-side stop to let him know that we were watching him. Anyway, I clocked your guy sitting in the passenger seat. If you ask me he stands out like a sore thumb.'

'Why do you say that? What happened? Is his cover blown?'

'No, he held it together. A bit over dramatic with my sergeant towards the end to be honest, but I'll think his cover is still safe, for now. Anyway, time to get all bud-dy-buddy; I need to know the extent and scope of your operation now, and we need to ensure that we don't tread on each other's toes and potentially fuck up both operations.'

'Okay, fair enough I guess. Right, where to start…'

'At the beginning always works for me.'

'Indeed, well, it won't be a surprise to you to know that the country is currently awash with drugs, and I mean liter-ally swimming in them. We haven't seen this level of import and distribution for, well, probably twenty-five years, since the rave scene in the late eighties and early nineties, when ecstasy was being swallowed by millions of club-goers like they were chocolate smarties. We have heroin that originates from Afghanistan, it follows a transit route through Turkey or Pakistan, and on through the Balkans. We have cocaine, primarily imported from Columbia and shipped into Spain, then finds its way in the UK via Antwerp or Rotterdam. Then we have ecstasy, originating from Holland back in the eighties and nineties, but more often manufactured across Eastern Europe now. This arrives on our shores by, well, bloody any route – boat, train, car. Finally, and less of a concern than the others, although the volume continues to increase year on year, is cannabis. We get resin coming from Afghanistan and Morocco, and herbal skunk coming from Holland and the Caribbean.'

Coker took a pause and a sip of his beer, which allowed Priest to get a few words in.

'I get the bigger picture, and I'm not naïve to the challenges we have trying to close our borders to import, and to tackle the onward distribution, but what's the direct relevance to the Dolsen crew and specifically your undercover officer? Accepting of course that they are known to be distributing drugs across the North West of England.'

'The Serious Organised Crime Agency set up a dedicated task force three years ago, to tackle the distribution of drugs across the North West, and in turn to take down the top two gangs moving the most volume.'

'Why only the top two? Surely there are a dozen or so major players across the North West?'

'That's where the definition of *major players* becomes somewhat subjective. Trust me, if we took out both the Yardies and the Dolsen family, we would remove over sixty percent of the drugs that currently flow through the North West.'

'And then no doubt other gangs would step in and fill the gap, and in time, based on the needs of natural supply and demand, the problem would be back to where it was, I assume?' Priest enquired.

'Correct,' confirmed Coker, 'it will be a continual battle.'

Both men briefly reflected on the long-term insignificance of their current activities whilst they took a few gulps of their beer.

'So, as I previously told you, we managed to get an undercover officer, Officer Darby, in place about thirteen months ago, and yes this will probably have been the guy you saw in the car with Shaun Dolsen, earlier this morning.'

'Is your officer able to provide any inside intel in support of our murder investigation?'

'I'll ensure that he gets the message next time he checks in, but his priority is nailing the Dolsen family for drug import and distribution.'

'Hmmm, not sure I agree on what his priorities should be considering we have a potential tit-for-tat gang war on our hands, but we'll agree to disagree for now.'

'Look, he's our guy, he works for SOCA and not the local CID, and his priorities will be aligned to what we want them to be. We will, of course, try and support your investigation with intel where possible.'

Nicola was to be found sitting on the sofa with a rather large glass of red wine when Priest entered.

'Hi, Nic.'

'Jonny, there's plenty left in the bottle. It's over there,' she pointed towards the half-empty bottle of Châteauneuf-du-Pape on the coffee table adjacent to him. There was a spare glass too. He picked it up and smiled at her.

'Always thinking of you, Jonny, always thinking of you.'

He poured a glass of an equally colossal measure and positioned himself on the sofa. Nicola raised her legs and placed them across his lap. They chinked their glasses to a coordinated 'cheers' and both settled their eyes towards the television.

'What are you watching?'

'Some US crime drama,' she confirmed.

'I don't know how you can watch this stuff, Nic.'

'This stuff?'

'Yes, you know, crime dramas. I mean, it's our life, it's our job. Do you not want to come home and switch off from it; and watch...you know...'

'What? You mean like David Attenborough documentaries on the Ugandan mountain gorilla, and the ecological and environmental impact made by gorilla excrement on the Rwenzori Mountains?'

'What?' Priest was a little bewildered. 'That doesn't even make sense.'

Nicola took a sip of her wine. 'I know. Anyway, I like my crime dramas, especially the US ones.'

There was a lull for a minute or two as their eyes settled back to the television.

'Rwenzori Mountains?' said Priest.

'Yes, Rwenzori Mountains,' she confirmed.

Sometime later Priest was woken by the sound of the telephone ringing. He looked down at his glass to see that he had finished his wine, then looked over towards Nicola, who was still absorbed by the crime drama that he recalled was just starting when he had taken his seat some time ago.

'I must have fallen asleep, sorry.'

'Yes, Jonny, you did. It's okay, although I had to knock you two or three times to stop you from snoring.'

'Snoring?'

'Yes, you were louder than the television. I kept turning up the volume to try and drown out your snoring, but every time I did, it got louder too. It was like you were in a subconscious competition with the television.'

He looked down at his wine glass. 'At least I finished my wine before I fell asleep.' He sounded pleased with himself, although for reasons probably only known to him.

'No, Jonny, you didn't. You fell asleep after about fifteen minutes and I took the wine from you to stop you from dropping the glass.'

'Ah, okay. Where did the wine go then?' Priest immediately realised the stupidity of the question when she turned towards him with a thick cheesy smile.

'Are you going to answer the phone then?'

'No,' replied Priest, just as it stopped anyway.

Then the muffled sound of 'Ride of the Valkyries' could be heard through Priest's trouser pocket as his mobile phone now sprung into life. He extracted it from his pocket. No caller ID. He chose not to answer.

As soon as the mobile had stopped ringing, the landline started again.

'Someone really needs to get hold of you, Jonny. You had better get it.'

He unravelled Nicola's legs that were still draped over his, and pulled himself up from the sofa. 'Hello,' Priest said as he looked at his watch; nine o'clock.

'Hello.' The voice on the other end was faint and crackly. 'Hello,' she said again.

'Yes, hello.'

'Oh, hello, is that Jonathan?' He hadn't been called by his full correct name for as long as he could remember.

'Yes, who is this?'

'Oh, Jonathan, this is your Auntie Joan.'

'Auntie Joan?' Priest was somewhat surprised to say that least; he hadn't seen or spoken to his auntie for well over ten years. It must be bad news; perhaps his Uncle Tony had passed away?

'I've been trying to reach you for hours, love, are you alright?'

'Yes, Auntie Joan, I'm fine thank you. Are you? What's prompted your call? Is everything okay with Tony? And you?'

'Yes, my love, we are both well; but I've got some bad news for you, Jonathan. You might want to sit down, love.' Priest wasn't the kind of person who needed to sit down to receive bad news; hardly likely to faint or collapse, he had been hardened by his job to almost all kinds of *bad news*, but he humoured his auntie nevertheless.

'I'm sitting down, Auntie Joan. Now what's this bad news?'

'I'm afraid it's your mum, love, she's passed away.' Now, hardened as Priest was to receiving and sometimes giving this type of news, it was a shock and it instantly took his breath away. Losing your parents is a natural progression of life, and society doesn't expect middle-aged adults to have an excessively emotional reaction to the loss of a parent. However, the loss of the first of your two parents is generally accepted to be much harder to bear; the actuality and finality confirming your parents aren't immortal and won't be around forever, tends to hit home and take most people by surprise. He took a few seconds to compose himself.

'When did it happen? How, and where?'

Nicola sat bolt upright; she knew that something was wrong.

'Early this morning, love; by all accounts she passed peacefully in her sleep.'

'Okay. Where's Dad?'

'He's at home, love, he's got Uncle Tony and a few others with him at the minute. Your dad's doing okay, putting on a brave face, you know.'

Priest didn't have the best of relationships with either his mother or his father. He hadn't spoken to his father for almost ten years, and had only sporadically spoken to his mother, perhaps a swift two minutes over the phone on her birthday and Christmas Day. He could easily and quickly recall what had triggered the fallout with his father a decade ago, but knew that his distant relationship with his mother was borne from the fallout and Priest's apparent, so he would later come to understand, inability to concede that he had been wrong, accept the blame, and to apologise.

'Thanks for letting me know, Auntie Joan.'

'You're welcome, my love. Will you be coming back, from wherever it is you live these days?'

'Manchester. I'm up in Manchester now, and yes I guess so. I'm sure I'll see you soon, and thanks again for letting me know.'

'Aright, love, you take care. Bye, bye.'

Priest placed the phone down and Nicola walked over to wrap her arms around him. They stood holding each other for five minutes. Nicola looked up at him. 'Are you okay?'

'Yes, babe, I'm fine. I'm going to have to call Superintendent Sawden, I might need a day or two off.'

CHAPTER 10

U ndercover SOCA officer Simon Darby wasn't at all apprehensive about his invitation to join Shaun and Davey at the Avenue club. He had slowly but surely gained the trust of higher echelons of the Dolsen family and particularly that of Shaun, who had already confided in him that tonight's meeting was to discuss the details of their proposed attack on the Yardies in revenge for the murder of Victoria.

Darby had arrived just before nine o'clock, as instructed. He wandered through to the VIP area where he found Shaun, Davey, Christopher and two others he knew only by their nicknames, Gibbo and Digger, the latter having been given his nickname on account of allegedly putting more people in the ground in the Greater Manchester area over the last five years than the Cooperative Funeral Service.

'You're late.'

Darby knew that he wasn't, but capitulated without hesitation as any attempt to challenge Davey would have no doubt gone down like a lead balloon. 'Yes, sorry, Davey.'

'Right, now that we are all here...' Noting that the three soldiers were unlikely to have been brought into the circle of confidence up to this point, Davey commenced to outline the reason for their meeting.

'We're having revenge on those fuckers, and we're having it soon.'

'What did you have in mind? What's the plan then?' asked Christopher.

'We're going to take out Ezekiel.' The others, whilst bloodthirsty and eager for revenge, sat back and pondered for a few seconds at the enormity of what they were contemplating. Ezekiel was a face across the North West, a member of the Yardies and someone to be avoided at all costs; unless that is, you were the Dolsen gang looking for some payback.

'Ezekiel?'

'Yes.'

'Well, that's going to send the right fucking message for sure.'

'How are we going to get near him, Davey, you know, without starting fucking World War Three at the same time?'

'We're going to snatch him tomorrow night outside that club they own; the VooDoo Lounge, you know, the one on Tennant Street.'

'Snatch him; I thought we were going to fucking waste him?'

'We are,' confirmed Davey, 'but I want to torture the fucker within an inch of his life first.'

'Ah fuck me, why can't we just shoot the fucker? How the fuck are we going to drag a six-foot-seven bodybuilder into the back of a fucking car whilst he's still alive and kicking? You're off your head, Davey.'

Davey reached behind the sofa and pulled a gun from within a plastic bag. 'With this.'

'I thought we weren't going to shoot him?'

'We aren't. This is a tranquiliser gun, it looks like a nine mill' pistol but it shoots darts, tranquiliser darts.' He reached into the bag and pulled out what looked like a rigid silver pencil case; he placed it on the table in front, opened the top and turned it around to show them.

'These three darts are filled with some kind of sedation liquid that will knock out your victim.'

'Excellent,' piped up Christopher for the first time, 'I've seen these on television, they're fucking awesome. One pop in the neck and they fall to the floor instantly.'

'Yes, although the reality, Christopher, is somewhat different. The guy that I got these from says forget the shit that you've seen on TV, the sedative will no doubt enter the body intramuscularly and is likely to take up to fifteen minutes to take effect.'

'Intra-what? That can't be right, Davey; it happens immediately on the TV.'

'Yeah well, the TV is bollocks. The guy tells me that unless you are injecting directly into a vein, the thirty seconds it would take for that to be effective will more likely be fifteen minutes.'

'So we need to get it into a vein then?'

'Yes, ideally I suppose, but I had planned on shooting him from a distance, not jabbing him up close.'

Darby piped up for the first time with a pragmatic comment. 'So once he's been darted, we just need to hold him down until the sedative takes effect.'

'Correct, and keep him quiet. He will have his full faculties, although I dare say these will diminish over the following minutes, plus he'll have a sabig fuck off gun on him, I bet, so we need to ensure we find that first and take control of it.'

The next forty minutes were spent discussing further details, with Davey confirming that this would all take place around eleven o'clock tomorrow night, in a side street adjacent to the club where Ezekiel was known to park his car. To the others that were listening, Davey projected a knowledge of Ezekiel and his movements that appeared to have been gained over a period of months, and not the two weeks since their sister had been killed. Perhaps this had been in the back of his mind for some time, and Victoria's murder was simply the catalyst he had been waiting for? Either way it didn't matter, revenge was on the cards and the Yardies had to pay, in blood.

Areas of responsibility were allocated, and the plan agreed before the club opened. What wasn't discussed, let alone agreed, was what they should do with Ezekiel once they had him. The allocated driver, Gibbo, had simply been told to drive to a lockup garage that Davey owned, some six miles away on the Oldham road.

The undercover cop, Darby, had been given a role too. Davey had asked him to carry the tranquiliser gun, and fire the dart into their intended victim. He had been given an important role, a key role, which reflected his growing trust from the brothers. He had readily accepted his part, of course he had, but he had a key decision to make, one that would define and potentially cement his undercover role, or might ultimately bring the whole case crashing down around them in a few months' time should they ever arrest the Dolsen family and proceed to court.

Darby's heart was telling him that he had to play along, he had to play his role in this potential abduction, which might itself lead to the murder of this Ezekiel guy. That act alone would be enough to send Davey to prison for twenty years, let alone the case they were trying to build for drugs trafficking and distribution. Yes, he had to play the short game where Davey could be implicated in this abduction and potential murder, but the long game was to further entrench Darby within the hierarchy of the gang; to reach a point whereby they trusted him and would speak freely in his presence. And Jimmy; Jimmy still needed to be implicated in something huge. If Ezekiel was abducted, beaten up and set free, the long game was still needed.

Darby's head, on the other hand, was eager to remind him that he was a police officer, and even undercover officers had rules, regulations, processes, protocols, and more importantly, lines that they could not cross. These *lines* were generally defined as *not breaking the law*, although in reality this was utter bollocks and almost impossible to adhere to. For most experienced undercover officers, this work was relatively black and white, these decisions fell into two categories. Firstly, there were actions that they could absolutely not undertake or participate in under any circumstances; murder would be the obvious one. However, if it didn't fall into the category of *absolutely not under any circumstances* then they would, in the main, retain the integrity of their cover and do what was necessary.

After wrestling with his conscience, albeit for all of thirty minutes, Darby decided he had more to gain than lose, so he was in. Davey had clearly already expected his compliance, so was somewhat nonplussed after hearing Darby's commitment to the plan, and acceptance of the part that he was to play.

As time marched on, the club started to fill and Darby lost sight of the others. He hadn't been required to work the door tonight, on account of the earlier meeting, so he had a free night. He chose to work; his police work.

'Alright, Chris,' Darby acknowledged one of the doormen as he exited the club, cigarette in hand. He walked twenty metres down the road and under the canopy of the rear exit of one of the fast food outlets, and extracted his mobile phone from the rear pocket of his jeans. The number he dialled was not stored in his contact list, he couldn't take that chance. The call was answered promptly.

'Hello.'

'Guv, it's Darby.'

'Darby, what's happened?' There was no set routine for Darby to check in. Ideally he had been asked to call and provide an update twice a week, but in reality most weeks he only managed a quick call once a week. He lived alone, and had plenty of time to check-in, but it was mainly apathy that led to his less than frequent calls. He had never called at eleven o'clock in the evening though, and Darby was relieved that DI Coker had his phone switched on.

'I've got some information that I need to share with you.'

'Okay, sounds promising, go on.'

'Davey Dolsen and some of the other lads are planning to abduct one of the Yardies tomorrow night. It's a guy called Ezekiel. We plan on abducting him in a road adjacent to the VooDoo Lounge at around eleven o'clock.'

'We plan…?'

'Yes, guv, I'm supposed to be part of the team that abducts him.'

'Well you can't, obviously.'

'No fucking shit,' came the rapid and rather terse reply, 'that's why I've called you. Clearly you need to intercept this tomorrow night, whilst somehow leaving me and the Dolsens untouched.'

'That's not going to be easy.'

'I know.'

'And this is going down when?'

'Tomorrow night at roughly eleven o'clock.'

'Shit, it doesn't give us much time. Maybe...'

'Maybe what?' Darby asked. There was a brief pause before DI Coker responded.

'Nothing, it doesn't matter.' Coker had, for the briefest of minutes, pondered on whether to do anything at all. If they did act on this information, Darby's cover might be compromised, and they might lose some or all of the traction they had gained in gathering evidence against the Dolsens, in fact they might blow the whole case against the gang, and for what? They were going to bundle a guy into the back of a car, drive him somewhere and beat him up. Was that a trade-off Coker was prepared to make in order to protect his investigation? No, of course it wasn't. Coker was all too aware that this Yardie was unlikely to be simply beaten up. Whilst SOCA's remit and focus was clearly on breaking up the illegal drug infrastructure across the North West, Coker was close enough to both his own case, and the multiple murder case being managed by Priest, to know that the Dolsens were after revenge, and that was headed down a one-way street; murder.

Despite that, he chose to grill Darby a little further. 'So what's the rest of the plan then?'

'What do you mean?'

'What do I mean? For fuck sake, Darby. What do you know about who's involved? What vehicles are the Dolsens taking? Where is this Ezekiel guy going to be taken? And more importantly, what are their intentions when they've got this guy in some bloody abandoned warehouse in the middle of nowhere? I assume the plan is to kill him, right?'

'To be honest, I don't know if Davey plans to kill him, or simply beat him up. They've been talking about revenge for Victoria's murder, but nothing specific was discussed about what would happen once we had him back at the lock-up.'

'The lock-up?'

'Yeah, some lock-up down Oldham Road. I don't know it, I've never been. Gibbo is to take him to the lock-up, then wait for Davey, I assume.'

'And what part are you going to play in all this?'

'You wouldn't believe me if I told you.'

'Well, I'm asking, so try me. What are you going to do, shoot him?'

The phone fell silent for a few seconds. 'Yes.'

'Yes, what do you mean, fucking yes?'

'Well, yes and no. I have been given a pistol to shoot him, but it's a tranquiliser gun. The plan is to drug him, to sedate him, and then bundle him into the back of Gibbo's car.'

'You do realise that it takes…' Coker was interrupted by Darby, 'yeah, we had that conversation already. I know.'

'Right, Darby, leave it with me, clearly we do need to intercept. This isn't a minor incident that can be overlooked. If there is any update or new information over the next twenty-four hours, you'll need to find a way to let me know.'

'Understood, guv.'

CHAPTER 11

The vibration of her mobile phone on the bedside cabinet alerted DS Stephens that she had received a text message. She rolled over towards the cabinet, picked it up and rubbed the haziness from her sleepy eyes. It wasn't from Jonny, as she had expected, but a message from the station. It read simply: *meeting with Superintendent Sawden 08:00hrs, v.important, move all other commitments to attend.*

She closed the message and looked at the time; five thirty-four. Her knee-jerk response to seeing the time was to question *who the bloody hell is in the office sending messages for the boss at half past five in the morning?* There was no way she would stand a chance of getting back to sleep now, so she tossed the covers back and bounded out of bed; well as much as she was able to bound, pre-six a.m.

'Good morning, Margaret, are we okay?'

'Ah, good morning, Sergeant Stephens, I'm fine thank you.' Stephens was about to continue with the pleasantries and small talk, but Sawden's PA was in one of her own super-orderly, head-down focussed moods. 'He's already in, sergeant, and expecting you. Please go in.'

'Thanks, Margaret.' Just as she passed by, she asked, 'am I in trouble?'

'Trouble?' she repeated, 'I've no idea, sergeant, are you?' Margaret's reply came with the faintest hint of satirical humour…and then a big smile, which released some of the initial anxiety within.

'Sergeant,' Stephens was warmly greeted by Sawden, 'please take a seat.'

'Thank you, sir.'

'Sorry to drag you in so early.'

'That's fine, sir, I am normally in shortly after eight anyway, shift dependent.'

'Yes, precisely. Have you met DI Coker?' he asked, finally acknowledging the third party in the room.

'Yes, sir, briefly at the briefing a few days ago.' Stephens turned to DI Coker. 'Guv.' Immediately she started to berate herself for her response; *bloody hell, did I just say briefly at the briefing?*

'DCI Priest has needed to take some compassionate leave for a couple of days, so I've asked Sergeant Stephens to join us. DS Stephens will be responsible for our end of the operation, inspector.'

Operation? Stephens' ears pricked up. 'Operation, sir?'

DI Coker spent the next ten minutes recounting the conversation with his undercover officer, Darby, from last night. It was a bit of a no-brainer, and all three agreed that mounting an operation to prevent this abduction and inevitable murder was essential. What wasn't as easily agreed was who would lead the operation. DI Coker, claiming both seniority and the fact that he had an undercover officer, an officer that would actually be present at the scene, claimed there was only one choice; it was SOCA, and it would be him.

Considering her limited experience discussing operational strategy at this senior level, DS Stephens did an admirable job in arguing that SOCA were a specialist unit whose remit here was, and should be, limited to illegal drugs, and that if SOCA did not have an active operation on the same characters, this would be a fairly routine operation for the CID team.

Superintendent Sawden agreed with her argument in principle, but then promptly confirmed that DI Coker should lead the operation, albeit a joint operation where the resources would mainly come from the local CID team, supported by uniformed officers from his station. Coker agreed.

'I've brought my sergeant with me, can we get started on the planning immediately?'

'Of course,' confirmed Sawden, 'can you find your way to the CID squad room, and Sergeant Stephens will be along shortly.'

'Of course.' And with that, DI Coker left the room.

'Sergeant, I wondered if you had heard from Chief Inspector Priest?'

'I haven't spoken to him this morning, sir, but I'm sure he's fine.'

'Gone back to London for a couple of days, I understand?'

'Yes, sir.' Stephens was unsure how much Priest had told him, and how much she should divulge herself, so she chose a minimalist approach. 'Family bereavement, sir. He's gone back for a couple of days to sort a few things out, but he'll be back at the weekend.'

'His mother, I hear.'

'Yes, sir.'

'Terrible business, sergeant.'

'Indeed, sir.'

'Okay. Between you and Sergeant Baxter, you'll keep the ship afloat, won't you?'

'Indeed, sir.' Stephens left his office wondering why he had mentioned DS Baxter; *bloody boys brigade.* Anyway, it didn't matter, there was an important operation to be planned for later that evening and she wanted to ensure that the CID team, her CID team today, were ready and wouldn't let DCI Priest down.

Thankfully it was a mild evening, and although the setting of the sun had taken away any heat, the night hadn't yet taken hold and the residual warmth was being enjoyed by all.

Between DI Coker and DS Stephens, they had decided that tonight's operation would require half a dozen uniformed officers, four plainclothes officers from the CID team, plus four officers from the Armed Response Vehicle. The ARV was positioned about one hundred metres away, and would be the primary unit to tackle the Dolsens. Everyone had been fully briefed on the details provided by Darby, including the probable involvement of a gun, and irrespective of it potentially only being a tranquiliser gun, no-one was going to take any chances, and the ARV was preparing as though it was going to be a real firearm.

DI Coker and DS Stephens were sitting in an unmarked squad car with direct line of sight of the VooDoo Lounge, and the adjacent road where the abduction was supposed to go down. The time was approaching ten-forty.

'Right, let me see if we are all awake.' Coker picked up his police radio. 'This is sierra one; all call signs radio check.'

'Sierra two confirm.' Sierra two was the ARV.

'Sierra three confirm.' Sierra three was DS Baxter, who was sitting at a window table in the kebab shop immediately across from the club.

'Sierra four confirm.' Sierra four was DC Stacey Wright and DC Simkins. They were positioned right outside of the club. Simkins was leaning up against the wall with his arms wrapped around Wright as she nestled her head in his chest; all whilst keeping an eagle eye out.

'Sierra five confirm.' Sierra five, finally, was the constable leading the half a dozen uniformed officers that were waiting fifty metres to the north of Coker's position.

'Okay, assuming it goes down as planned, we should expect our Yardie to arrive in the next fifteen to twenty-five minutes, which means that the Dolsens should be arriving and parking up, waiting for him, sometime in the next five to ten. Keep your eyes peeled, and check in if you see anything.'

No-one knew what they were keeping their eyes peeled for. They had no intelligence on the vehicle that the Dolsens would be driving; they were aware of the vehicles that were owned and registered to the family and most of the gang members, but it was thought highly unlikely that they would attempt this in one of their own vehicles that could so easily be traced back to the family. No, they were waiting for Ezekiel to arrive and park his car in the side road, then an expected squeal of tyres as another car came to a grinding halt before multiple men charged out towards him. Well, that was what was expected.

The minutes passed; five, ten, fifteen. Little happened, until a black Range Rover pulled up outside of the club and reversed into the adjacent street.

The respective radios and discreet earpieces crackled into life. 'That's our guy, keep your eyes peeled and move on my mark only,' announced Coker. When Coker announced, *that's our guy*, it was a massive assumption that the guy in the Range Rover was actually Ezekiel. It could have been just about anyone. In the preceding few hours, CID had been unable to verify his identity and find a photograph of him, even the DVLA didn't have a driving licence for him, current or expired. The fact was that Coker had simply made the assumption that this guy must be Ezekiel, because Darby had told him that he would arrive at the VooDoo Lounge at eleven o'clock. Anyway, it had been discussed and agreed that it really didn't matter that they didn't know what Ezekiel looked like; they were actually looking and waiting for the Dolsens to come into the picture at some point.

Everyone was looking around them, looking for groups of men coming out of the shadows, parked cars ready to hurtle forwards. They scanned the few groups, or individuals, that were on the streets but no-one looked like they might be ready to make a move. They were all Joe Public just going about their business.

They waited, and waited, but nothing was happening.

The tension in the air was palpable and the adrenalin had certainly kicked in now. DS Baxter had risen from his seat inside the kebab shop, and had walked outside to light a cigarette. Between Baxter, Simkins and Wright, there were three CID officers within twenty metres of the front of the club as Ezekiel exited his car. A quick press of his key fob and his car was locked, and he started to walk back up towards the main road.

'Can anyone see anything? Has anyone got eyes on Dolsen?'

'No.'

'No.'

'Negative.'

'No, guv.' They all sounded off one by one; no-one had visibility of Dolsen, his crew, or where they were likely to come from. Time was running out.

Within ten seconds, Ezekiel had reached the front door of the club. He shook hands with the two of the three doormen, then disappeared inside.

'Shit!' exclaimed DI Coker.

'What's happening, guv?' asked Simkins via the radio.

'Nothing. Something's happened, they've been scared off, or tipped off somehow.'

Coker looked across to Stephens and puffed out his cheeks. 'Bollocks! What do you think, sergeant?'

'I agree, guv, something spooked them, or they were never here, called it off at the last minute, as you said. But...'

'But?'

'Well, to be honest, the operation has been a bit of a blowout, but we did actually achieve our primary objective; to prevent the Dolsens from abducting Ezekiel.'

'Yes, I guess you're right, and my officer hasn't blown his cover in the process. I hope.'

They waited a further fifteen minutes before Coker called off the operation. 'Okay, let's debrief tomorrow morning back at the station. Thanks, all, sorry it was a waste of time.'

CHAPTER 12

It was the day of Victoria Dolsen's funeral, three weeks since her death, and the day couldn't have come a moment too soon according to Priest. He knew that the Dolsens were still looking for some kind of revenge or retribution, despite the fact that Victoria's murder was revenge itself for the earlier murder of the Yardie, Jarel Lamar Powel, although Priest wasn't aware of this yet. This was the next event that had to be completed in order to make some progress back towards normality. Superintendent Sawden had called Victoria's funeral one of the milestones that needed to be achieved.

Milestones? thought Priest; he wasn't project managing some IT deployment somewhere, *fucking milestones!*

Victoria's boyfriend, Johannes De Groot, was still in hospital, and under twenty-four-hour observation within the intensive care unit. Hs condition hadn't changed in the three weeks since he had been shot, and the prognosis remained bleak for him to awaken, let alone make any meaningful recovery.

Priest had chosen not to go to the station first; the church service was to commence at ten o'clock, followed by the committal service at the local crematorium at eleven-thirty. He would attend the latter.

After waking, and upon hearing the news that Jonny would not be leaving early for the station, Nicola had thought that they might spend an extra hour in bed making love, before showering and spending a further hour on a leisurely breakfast, like a normal couple. It wasn't to be. Jonny needed 'to think and clear my head' so he advised that he would be strapping on his Nikes and venturing out for a 10K run.

Priest had arrived back home fairly late last night, and Nicola had purposely not kept him up to date with current activities whilst he was in London on compassionate leave. The thirty-minute drive to the All Saints Crematorium provided ample opportunity for Nicola to bring him up to speed on the kidnap plot that never transpired, and in turn Priest had, somewhat reluctantly, shared details of his brief time in London.

His two days in London had been spent doing just what had been expected of him. After calling to see his dad, which would have been a far frostier encounter were it not for the fact that Aunty Joan and Uncle Tony were there at the same time, he called to see his mum.

His visit to the chapel of rest was only supposed to be ten to fifteen minutes, but he found himself pulling up a chair and talking to her for almost an hour. He had taken an old black and white photo from his jacket pocket; the photo was of Jonny and his parents, taken when Jonny was six years old. The backdrop was Margate Pier, and they looked happy, arms wrapped around each other, standing on the pebble beach with the Kent sun beaming onto their backs. His dad was wearing a pair of corduroy trousers and a shirt, unbuttoned to the bottom. Mum was wearing a light coloured dress and sandals, and Jonny, well, Jonny was resplendent in just a pair of swimming trunks.

He slipped the photo into the coffin, leant over and kissed his mum on the forehead, and left. A tear came to his eye and he walked back to the car. He sat in the car for a few moments; he was pleased that he had seen his mum and had the opportunity to say goodbye, but he wouldn't be back again.

The funeral would be in a week's time.

Priest turned off the main road and into the crematorium. The building itself could not be seen from the road, and Priest started down a long smooth tarmac driveway that was lined every ten metres with the most gorgeous weeping willow trees whose golden leaves hung effortlessly from the branches, the branch tips themselves gently kissing the ground, swaying up and down as the light breeze caught them.

It was a good forty seconds before the crematorium came into view; the poignancy hadn't escaped either of them, especially at this difficult time for Priest. They both looked out of the windows, past the mature trees and beyond, into the acres of well-tended mature lawns and bedding areas. Priest imagined that this would be a pleasurable final journey, for those that had needed to experience it; albeit subconsciously…well, dead actually.

Priest briefly chuckled to himself.

'What?' asked Nicola.

'Nothing, it's nothing.' After a few seconds, he chuckled again.

'Come on, out with it. What can possibly have made you laugh driving down towards the crematorium?'

'I was just thinking about a sat nav.'

'A what? Why?'

'Well, if you didn't know where the crematorium was, you might input the address at the start of your journey.'

'And?'

'Well, it occurred to me that as you drive down this road, the voice on the sat nav would probably say, you have reached your final destination.'

Nicola looked at him, gobsmacked. 'You're not funny, Jonny.'

The car came to a halt in the car park, and Priest checked the time; five past eleven. With the church service having finished five minutes ago, and the drive from the church to the crematorium being five to ten minutes, they could expect the first arrivals fairly soon.

The crematorium was a modern building. Architecturally unique, it wasn't like any other building that you might come across. You would never see houses built to look like this, or offices, hospitals, nursing homes, stately homes, leisure centres, supermarkets, shops, schools or barns. Crematorium designs were fairly unique and striking, and could be picked out in an instant in a selection of a dozen images of various builds. The closest comparison that Priest could make was a modern golf clubhouse, a single-storey structure, centre peak roof, with a protruding covered entrance area supported by two, if not four, stone pillars. The comparison was further supported by the meticulously manicured lawns and bedding areas as far as the eye could see. Yes, this looked like quite a few nineteenth holes Priest had frequented over the years.

After covertly attending the funeral of Jarel Powell three weeks ago, Priest had decided on a more overt attendance and visible presence this time, and with DS Stephens was standing next to the car when the first of the mourners' cars started to arrive. One by one, group by group, they parked their cars, and started to file through the front doors ahead of and waiting for the immediate family, chief mourners and the hearse.

As Priest watched the last of mourners enter, there was a lull in activity for a couple of minutes. 'Any minute now I would guess,' noted Priest. Stephens simply smiled her response. As Priest turned his head back, he saw the black hearse slowly driving down the tarmac road towards the crematorium building. Still a couple of hundred metres away, and with views across the open grounds behind, Priest saw four, five, six, black funeral cars trailing the hearse. The Dolsens had certainly come out in force this spring morning.

The hearse pulled up at the entrance, and two of the pallbearers exited and moved towards the rear, as the large rear door opened automatically and slowly. Whilst they waited to gain access to the coffin, the family and other chief mourners had exited the many cars behind and were standing patiently, waiting to follow the coffin inside.

Priest and Stephens were standing at a respectful distance, but still managed to catch the eye of Jimmy, Davey and Shaun Dolsen. Stephens commented on Davey's stare. 'Oooh, Jonny, if looks could kill?'

Priest smiled back at her and briefly chuckled, 'not sure about looks capable of killing, but for sure everyone in that family has the means and motivation to kill.'

Davey took a step forward out of the line that had started to form, as though he was going to walk towards their position, but any intent was quickly thwarted by Jimmy as he grabbed hold of his arm. Much to his annoyance, which he had no qualms in projecting, Davey fell back into line again, for now.

As the coffin entered the crematorium, followed by the family and mourners, Priest looked over his shoulder. He had no idea what had prompted him to do so, a sixth sense no doubt. His gaze took him to the immediate horizon, which was a collection of half a dozen trees about two hundred metres away, where he saw two men partially hiding behind the heavy trunks of the mature trees. They were not trying to be completely inconspicuous, but clearly neither did they want to announce their presence.

Due to their obvious focus elsewhere, it was highly unlikely that the Dolsens had noticed them, but Priest had. One of them was Sergeant Thomas, of that there was no doubt. The dishevelled look of two weeks' facial stubble combined with a head of wiry black curls that was so desperately in need of a date with a pair of clippers, was unmistakable even though Priest had only met him the once. The other looked like Constable Winstanley; both officers were from DI Coker's team, the Serious Organised Crime Agency.

It took about twenty seconds, and Priest wouldn't avert his gaze, but Sergeant Thomas eventually acknowledged him with a brief waft of his hand.

'Are you going over to talk to them?' asked Stephens, who had also clocked who they were.

'No, I don't think so. I was half expecting to see them here, to be honest. There's nothing like a crime family funeral to bring all the knowns and unknowns into plain sight. The opportunity to finally lay eyes on someone you have only heard about, or to confirm suspected friendships and affiliations is generally an opportunity not to be missed. But no, I'll leave them alone to do their own thing, whatever that is.'

'They might have brought sandwiches,' said Stephens.

'What? Sandwiches? What are you talking about?' asked a perplexed Priest.

'You know, they might have been here for a couple of hours already, and are settling in for a couple more, they might have a satchel with a picnic inside. They might have it all laid out on a navy tartan picnic rug. They might be sharing a foot-long sausage roll.' She started to laugh at herself, unable to keep it up any further.

'You're off your bloody head, Nic.' Priest returned his focus to the crematorium, just as the last of the mourners entered the building, so Priest and Stephens decided to retire inside their car.

'Should only be about twenty to twenty-five minutes I think.'

'Are we staying then?' asked Stephens.

'Yes, I thought we might.'

'Why?'

'We are paying our respects.'

'No we're not, or we would be inside, or we would have attended the church service. What are we going to do for twenty-five minutes?'

'I spy with my little eye, something...'

'Shut up, you muppet; I'm thirty-nine years old. I'm not playing I spy with my boss, whilst sitting in a police car outside of a crematorium.'

Priest looked at her, somewhat overly perturbed by her response. 'Spoilsport.'

Shaun Dolsen was the first familiar face to show as the double doors were opened, and held so, by one of the crematorium ushers. His eyes were immediately drawn towards Priest, and it was obvious he was heading their way.

'Head up, Nic, here we go.' Priest got out of the car, and was standing by the door as Shaun approached him.

'What the fuck are you doing here?' Dolsen's body language and aggressive posturing would have seen him thrown out of any one of their nightclubs, were his behaviour to manifest in anyone else.

'We are just paying our respects to your sister, Shaun.'

'You've got no business being here, you're not wanted. Just fuck off.'

'Now, that's not very nice is it, especially on a day like today.'

'Fuck off.'

'Charming use of vocabulary, Shaun. Have you got any other verbal delights, to be asserted again with such vociferous resolve, that you would like to convey?'

Shaun, clearly perplexed by Priest's purposeful tongue-twisting answer, only had the one response. 'Fuck off.'

'Look. There is an open investigation, looking to find the person, or persons, responsible for Victoria's death. We are just trying to ensure they are found, and justice is…' He was cut short.

'Is what? And you think that you might find the killer here, amongst us, amongst our family and friends, the mourners? We've told you before, copper, we don't need your help in finding out who killed our sister, and we sure as hell don't need your help in what happens after that.'

'That'll do, Shaun.' Jimmy Dolsen had walked over to where they were. 'That'll do. Don't say anything else.'

Shaun shrugged off Jimmy's hand that was placed on his shoulder, and turned to walk away, still chuntering something less audible now, and no doubt just to himself.

'Please accept my apologies, chief inspector, my brother is rather highly strung and gets quite emotional, especially when he is burying one of his siblings.' And with that, and without waiting for any reply or further verbal engagement, Jimmy also turned on his heels to join his family and friends.

'Time to leave?' asked Stephens.

'I guess so,' came the reply.

CHAPTER 13

I t had taken Shaun Dolsen almost five hours to drive to London; South Lambeth to be precise. He had travelled down with Terry Woolhouse, and had found the journey to be fairly challenging to say the least. Woolhouse was one of the family's most trusted foot soldiers who had served them for ten or more years, but by God he was clearly a pork pie short of a picnic, and as Davey had eloquently noted once, *when God was handing out brains, Woolhouse thought he said trains, and missed his.*

Shaun had found the conversation taxing but had persevered, and by the time they were a few miles from their destination, their sporadic conversations had swung from debating the pros and cons of pale ale versus lager, to a leisurely verbal wander through IKEA flat pack furniture, and ultimately ended up trying to outdo each other on *the best and worst places I've ever had sex.* Apparently *on the roof of a seven-storey hotel in Rhodes* marginally pipped *inside a cave at Matlock Bath* to the prize of the best place. Although Shaun literally had no response to the worst place when he heard that Terry had broken into an abattoir when he was nineteen, and had taken his girlfriend up against a skinned and gutted pig, suspended by a hook from an overhead rail.

'She fucking loved it,' he said, 'she was into all that weird shit anyway.'

'Right.'

'Trust me, she didn't take much persuading.'

'Really? And how long after your abattoir session did you split up?'

'Who says we broke up?'

'Me. How long?'

'Yeah, okay, about a week I think.'

'Enough said.'

The female voice from the satellite navigation system in Shaun's Range Rover politely announced that they were four miles from their destination, and a quick check of the time showed them to be two hours early. Shaun wasn't known for being early for anything, in fact if anyone was to be late it would be Shaun. This was different, this was an important meeting and being late just wouldn't cut it today.

'Let's pull in here for a couple of jars,' announced Shaun as he pulled the car to the side of the road, having spied a pub.

Woolhouse got out and looked up at the façade. 'The Crown and Anchor; what a fucking shithole.'

To be fair, the Crown and Anchor had seen better days, well, at least the outside had. It was lacking in kerbside appeal, and was probably a head turner for all the wrong reasons.

'I'm sure it's much better inside,' said Shaun.

'I assure you, it can't be any worse than the outside,' noted Woolhouse, with a hint of trepidation as he looked to cross the threshold.

'Listen to you. Connoisseur and frequenter of refined public houses, with charm, elegance and a homely feel. You spend all of your time in fucking Wetherspoons, what do you know about sophisticated boozers?'

'I don't need sophistication, Shaun, just somewhere that I'm not likely to be bitten by fucking rats whilst I have a pint.'

'Fair point. It'll do fine for an hour or so, come on, crack on.'

It was too early for the club to open, even for the Dolsen family, the owners, but it was never too early for a drink.

Darby had been in the Cock & Bull pub for almost two hours when Davey Dolsen strode through the door; he spied Darby over on the far side throwing some arrows with an old guy who was familiar to Davey. Just as Davey approached, Darby threw his third into the plywood that surrounded the dart board.

'Looks like you've got this young lad whipped, eh, Stan.'

'I'm letting him win,' interjected Darby.

'Sure you are. Looks like the only thing that you're doing is getting pissed and making holes in the fucking wall.'

'He's alright, Davey,' noted Stan, 'I'm keeping an eye on him.'

Davey placed a hand on Stan's shoulder. 'I'm sure you are, Stan, I'm sure you are. Pint of best, is it?'

Stan held aloft his half empty pint glass. 'Don't mind if I do, thanks, Davey.'

By the time Davey had arrived back from the bar with three pints, Stan had won the game after a finish of thirty-six, and Darby had successfully achieved double-top and two further holes in the eggshell anaglypta wallpaper.

'Cheers, young man.' Stan took the full pint with both hands.

'Have you got it?' asked Davey.

'Yes, Davey, thank you.'

'You're welcome, now be a good chap and bugger off over there whilst I have a chat with my man here.'

Stan picked up his pint that he had only just placed down on the table, and shuffled off towards the opposite side of the room.

'How long have you been out?' enquired Davey.

'Don't know, three, maybe four hours.'

'You need to slow down a bit.'

'Day off today, Davey. I've not been needed by Jimmy, I've not heard from you, and fuck knows where Shaun is, so I'm having a day of R&R.'

'Okay, let your hair down, have a few beers, but for fuck sake just slow down a bit.'

'I will, Davey.' Darby sensed that Davey needed appeasing. 'I will, I promise.'

'Good man. Look, why don't you come to the club later this evening? We'll crack some bubbly and find some tarts to entertain us.'

'Sure, why not?' confirmed Darby, 'I'm just going to meet a couple of lads for a catch up, and a couple of beers, and I'll see you there.'

Darby didn't know *a couple of lads*, he was an under-cover police officer with no social life, living, working and socialising with one of the North West's dangerous and most notorious drug gangs. He wanted to be alone. He wanted to be unsociable, he wanted his own space, and more than anything else, he wanted to leave these cretinous vermin and return to his normal life.

Undercover work had been an exciting draw two years ago, but it had taken its toll, and he wanted out. He needed out.

Shaun Dolsen had been ready for this meeting since it was initially agreed some three months ago. The meeting was supposed to have taken place last week but it had coincided with Victoria's funeral, and Shaun had managed to get them to agree to reschedule it. His request had initially been met with resistance until he had opened up further and advised them of the circumstances. *There's nothing more important than family* he was advised, and they agreed on today's date, although it was unlikely that any further proposed rescheduling would be tolerated.

Shaun rolled his Range Rover up to what appeared to be locked gates, but just as he approached, a man appeared from the shadows. The man, smartly dressed in a two-piece grey gingham check suit covered by a tailored Crombie overcoat, approached the driver's door. The window wound down and the two men looked at each other.

'The 1964 FA Cup final was an enjoyable game,' noted Shaun. The other man stood for a few seconds, absorbing the words he had just heard. *Mancunians*, he thought to himself, *I fucking hate Mancs.*

'It was a good game, but I remember it rained all day.'

The cryptic greeting had been agreed in advance as one of the security conditions set by Shaun's hosts. They even went so far as to advise that any error, misunderstanding, or anyone passing themselves off as Dolsen would be shot then gutted, or was it gutted then shot? Shaun couldn't recall. The guy opened the gates and pointed them in the direction of the main industrial unit forty metres ahead of them.

As they approached the unit, the large front doors slid open, just wide enough for Shaun to drive inside.

Shaun Dolsen had travelled to London to finalise a deal to secure a new pipeline for the supply of crack cocaine. He had arranged to meet Tommy Randles; Tommy was part of the Randles family, another white family gang who appeared to own much of the wholesale distribution south of the Thames, and certainly the east side.

Shaun and Tommy hadn't met before and the meeting had, in part, been initially brokered by a mutual acquaintance called Dom 'Clinton' Ashley. His nickname had taken some time to stick, having been earned as apparently he had sold more illegal weapons during the eight years that Clinton was US President, than the USA had legally exported. This fact was not strictly statistically correct obviously, but Ashley's peers, colleagues, customers, competitors and the criminal underworld as a whole were aware that he was the 'go-to' man for firearms; and it didn't matter if you lived in Lands' End or John O'Groats, if you needed to know Clinton, you knew Clinton. In the absence of this intermediary tonight though, the meeting could quickly go pear-shaped.

'Shaun?' A man in his mid-twenties stepped forward with his hand outstretched.

'Tommy?' Shaun took his hand.

'Welcome to London. Are you seeing any of the sights whilst you're down here?'

'Sights? No, Tommy, I've not come to look at fucking Big Ben, or to ride on that fucking big wheel near the river, and I'm sure as hell not going to be knocking on the doors of Buckingham Palace to see if the Queen wants to nip to the boozer for a jar or two.' Shaun clearly didn't do warm welcomes, and his interpersonal skills were devoid of, well, anything in the area of listening or communication.

'No, I guess not. Straight to business it is then.' Randles whistled and one of his guys appeared with a small package in his hand. He handed it to Randles, who in turn tossed it over to Shaun.

'What's this?'

'Let's call it a little gesture on my part, an investment in the potential longevity of our relationship.'

Shaun tossed it to Terry.

'So, ten kilos per month, rising to twenty-five kilos within six months if you can demonstrate that you can move that weight.'

'Don't worry about our side,' replied Shaun, 'I'm more concerned about you being able to supply that weight, month by month.'

He received nothing more than an indignant smile from Randles, and that is where Shaun really should have left it, but this *was* Shaun Dolsen.

'I mean, I'm not being funny, but look at you.' Shaun gestured with his outstretched hands towards Randles and his three colleagues. 'You're suited and booted like...I don't know, fucking stockbrokers or life insurance salesmen. I need to know that you can supply twenty-five kilos a month.'

'Young, transient and highly mobile, would be how the estate agents describe the young professional residents of this area. Affluent and well-heeled might be another. But we're none of the above, Mr Dolsen. We are not stockbrokers or life insurance salesmen. We are very much your modern day entrepreneurs, and you'd be wise not to fuck with us.'

'Modern day entrepreneurs?' Shaun started to laugh. Randles had reached the end of his already very short patience, and reached inside his long overcoat. He pulled out a Mac-10, quickly removed the safety catch and proceeded to fire a short burst of five rounds into the front driver's side tyre of the Range Rover, followed by a further three into the rear tyre. Both popped and flattened immediately.

'Underestimate us at your peril, Mr Dolsen.' He returned the firearm to the holster in his jacket, and everyone stood in silence for a few seconds just waiting for the tension to defuse, and to see if Shaun was going to do anything in return. He didn't.

'A little bit overdramatic; but your point has been well made.'

'First batch in ten days' time; we'll send you the time and venue.'

'Okay, we're in.' Randles wasn't expecting anything else.

Randles turned towards his vehicle, as did Dolsen, although the latter was somewhat unsure how he was going to move his.

'Wait here,' Randles advised, 'I'll have a guy come along within the next two hours. He'll put two new tyres on for you.'

'Two hours. Fuck me, I can probably have the RAC here in thirty minutes.'

'Take it or leave it.'

'Okay, I'll take it. Thanks.'

'Don't thank me yet, he will want paying, in cash, and by the look of those tyres it's going to cost you a monkey at least.' Randles chuckled to himself.

'Hi, Davey, how are you?' The hostess from the VIP area greeted Davey Dolsen with the same degree of enthusiasm as she had done all the other VIP guests that night. For some the evening was coming to a close, but at one o'clock in the morning, Davey's night was just about to begin. The club would start to wind down at two o'clock, but Davey wouldn't be ejected with the riff-raff; after all it was his family business.

'Hi Emily,' he greeted her with a peck on the cheek, 'how's business tonight?' The family in the main, although perhaps with the exception of Shaun, treated the staff very well. Some of the more senior staff that had been there and worked for the Dolsens for many years, were wise to the importance of the club to the family, and whilst they themselves probably knew very little about what happened behind closed doors, it was clear that the club had multiple areas of interest for the family. Hosting the cool, trendy and rich millennials of Manchester could be fun at times, but it was unlikely to be their primary interest.

'I'm very well thank you, Davey, and business has been pretty good tonight.'

'Good.'

'We've had every VIP table full all evening, and we have done more champagne and bottles of vodka than I've seen us sell for months.'

'Excellent.' Davey moved in to kiss Emily on the forehead. 'Well done; keep it up. I'll make sure Jimmy knows.'

'Thanks, Davey.'

Davey started to walk away, but was stopped in his tracks. 'Oh, Davey, sorry just one thing.'

'What?'

'I thought you should know. Darby is in one of the VIP booths, he's got a girl with him.'

'Do we know her?'

'Yes, she's a regular.'

'So…'

'Well, he's pissed, and I mean really pissed. If it were anyone else, I would have asked one of the lads to eject him.'

'Is he being abusive to the girls, or other customers?'

'Actually, no, he's not. He's just absolutely trolleyed,' she confirmed.

Davey immediately remembered that he had mentioned to Darby that they should meet in the club earlier that evening; although no specific time was agreed, Davey wondered if Darby had been there since the club had opened. 'Okay, thanks, Emily. Leave it with me.'

Davey took his drink that had been delivered to him by another hostess and walked around the VIP area until he found the booth where Darby was sitting. The booths were designed to provide a degree of privacy. They were open at the front, allowing access in and out of the seating area, but the high sides of the seats afforded some visual and audible privacy from others seated in booths either side. Davey had to walk past most of the booths until he found the one where Darby was seated.

'Darby.'

'Davey.'

The mutual greeting was nothing if not succinct and to the point.

'Who's the skirt?' The woman immediately appeared vexed, and looked over to Darby expecting him to step in and say something. She didn't get the response she was hoping for.

'This is…' he was visually struggling to recall her name, 'errr…sorry, what is your name?'

'Rachel. It's Rachel. I've been sitting here talking to you for over two hours, and you don't remember my name?'

Davey jumped in, short on time and patience as usual. 'You've been sitting here for almost three hours actually, during which time you have managed to consume at least three bottles of champagne, each of which costs one hundred and ninety-five pounds. And as it looks like my friend here is drinking his usual Jack Daniels and coke, I would surmise that you have enjoyed almost six hundred quid of free champagne tonight. The fact that my friend doesn't remember your name is a mixture of the volume of alcohol that he has clearly consumed, coupled with the fact that you are an instantly forgettable freeloader. Now fuck off.'

The woman immediately picked up her handbag from the seat, and left without saying a word.

'Bit harsh, Davey, but okay.'

'Trust me, you'll thank me for it later.'

'Something on your mind?' asked Darby, as he took another swig from his tumbler.

'There wasn't, until I arrived at the club.'

'Right. What's wrong?'

'You. I spoke to you earlier this afternoon in the Cock & Bull; you cannot get this pissed. It's not safe for the family, or for you come to think of it.'

'This is our club, Davey, it's a safe environment.'

'In the main, yes, but when you get this pissed you drop your guard. You might inadvertently say something that you shouldn't, you know, perhaps to impress a tart.'

'Ah, secrets, Davey. Secrets.'

'Kind of.' Davey watched Darby take another gulp and empty his tumbler. 'You really are fucking wrecked aren't you?'

'Not as pissed as you might tink; tank; thank, think.'

'Really?' Davey stood up. 'Right, I'm going to get one of the boys to call a taxi for you, okay?'

'Okay, Davey.'

Just as Davey started to walk away, Darby called him back. 'Davey, Davey.' He stopped and turned around. 'Talking about family secrets, I've got a secret that you don't know.'

'Goodnight, Darby, you're pissed. We'll see you tomorrow, perhaps some time after lunch I guess.' Davey started to walk away again.

'It's about that murdered Yardie.' Davey stopped. 'And it's about Shaun.' Now he turned back around.

'Be very careful what you say next, Darby.'

'Sit down and I'll tell you something.' Davey returned to the booth, and took a seat.

'You've got five minutes, and a very short piece of rope with which to hang yourself.'

'That Yardie that was killed six weeks ago, it was Shaun that killed him.'

'Bollocks.'

'I'm telling the truth, Davey.'

'Why should I believe you? And why the fuck would you know something like that? Shaun would have told me. Bollocks. What's your fucking game?'

'Why do I know? Why do I know? Because I was with him, Davey. I was with him.' Darby was slurring his words, but Davey picked up enough.

Davey was clearly stunned, and speechless for a few seconds, but ready to concede that there could be an element of truth here. 'Okay, tell me it all.'

'Firstly, this was clearly something that Shaun had been planning for a while.'

'How do you know?'

'Because, and I'll get to that point in more detail, after we had grabbed the guy, Shaun had all the gear in the back of the van, and he had obviously planned where he would take him, and what he would do when he got there.'

'What gear? Got where?' Davey was eager for details.

'Shaun called me one night, he said he needed an extra pair of hands for a job. I asked him what it was, but he was a bit evasive. Well, when I say a bit evasive, I mean absolutely secretive. He did say that it was family business, and that Jimmy was aware, so I went along. Long story short, that Saturday night we waited outside a house near Maine Road, and we grabbed the Yardie when he pulled onto his drive. It was surprisingly easy to be honest. We bundled him into the back of the van, and Shaun gave him an almighty twat on the head with the bat. That knocked him out.'

'Okay, then what did you do? Where did you go?'

'Shaun asked me to drive towards Oakwood Lane Woods, and when we got close, he guided me down a dirt track that took us deeper into the woods. I drove as far as I could, until we couldn't drive any further. I got out of the van, walked around to the rear and opened the doors, and Shaun had only gone and tied him up with some rope, head to toe. He looked like a fucking trussed up Christmas turkey.'

'He had tied him up whilst you were driving?'

'Yes, and that wasn't all. He had fucking stripped him bare.'

One of the VIP hostesses passed by and Davey took an opportunity to indicate their desire for another drink by waving the empty glass tumbler in the air with one hand, and holding two fingers up in the other.

'Tools or body, he asked me; dunno I said, upon which he pulled the body out of the van and onto his shoulders. He told me to pick up the holdall that was in the back and bring it, together with both sets of stepladders. I had no idea what was in the holdall, but this is where he must have been planning this for some time.'

Davey motioned for Darby to hold it there for a few seconds as there drinks were being delivered. 'Thanks, Kim.' The VIP hostess arrived and placed two drinks on the table.

'You're welcome, Davey.'

Davey took a couple of swigs from the glass tumbler, and took a long and purposeful exhale. 'Carry on.'

'Well, again to cut a long story short, Shaun carried the body and I carried the holdall and stepladders into the woods. I was following Shaun; he seemed to know exactly where he was headed. We walked for about fifteen minutes, and then stopped at a large tree, whereupon......'

Darby paused, but Davey egged him on; 'and...'

'Well, Shaun laid him out on the ground and placed his hands and feet together. I still didn't really have a clue what he was going to do; I had no idea why I had carried two sets of fucking stepladders hundreds of metres into the woods. Anyway, Shaun opened up the holdall and pulled out a hammer and two big nails, and I mean fucking massive nails, the kind of nails that you don't use for fucking DIY around the house.'

Davey dared not ask, but he did anyway. 'And what did he do?'

'He plunged the fucking nails straight through the guy's hands and feet.'

'Fuck me!'

'Indeed. Finally, with a bit of brute force and some awkward lifting and holding, hence the stepladders, we held the guy up right and Shaun drove the protruding six inches of nail straight through him and into the tree.'

Davey was lost for words. Shaun was known to have somewhat of a sadistic streak about him, but this topped all of his previous known exploits.

'To be honest, Davey, I'm surprised he stayed up there, you know, pinned to the fucking tree.'

'And…'

'Well, all I could think of was *Spartacus*.'

'What?'

'You know, that movie with Michael Douglas, about Romans and gladiators, and stuff.'

'It was Kirk Douglas, you moron, anyway forget bloody *Spartacus*. And…'

'And, nothing. We left, and Shaun told me not to mention it to anyone. He didn't want anyone in the family to know.'

'But you said, he told you that Jimmy was aware.'

'He had, when he initially called me, yes. However, whilst he was driving those fucking eight-inch nails into the tree, he let slip that he had lied, and that no-one knew. Just me, and him. What are you going to do, Davey?'

'Well I'm going to have to tell Jimmy for a start. He is going to go fucking ballistic.'

Darby left the club shortly after his confession to Davey. He poured himself into the back of a taxi, closed his eyes and let out an almighty exhale as his shoulders sagged down. It was as though his confession had lifted the weight of the world from his shoulders. He was relieved;

it was a heavy secret to have been carrying. But what now? What were to be the repercussions of his confession? Jimmy would be livid, of that there was no doubt. Shaun would be, well, God only knew. He would either look to revel in his notoriety, albeit within the relatively safe confines of the family, or he would be looking to dispatch a serious beating to Darby for betraying his trust and divulging their secret so easily. Either way, Darby felt a gush of relief, tinged with a dash of worry.

Having said that, Darby was only half unburdened. Sure, he had opened up to Davey, but that in itself was sure to have future repercussions that Darby could only hope wouldn't blow back on him through the Dolsen family. But what Darby hadn't done, was to inform his boss; his police boss. Funnily enough, participating in a crime of any sort, let alone a murder, is somewhat frowned upon when you are a serving police officer. This applies even more so to undercover officers. The days of the 1970s and 80s where police officers, especially undercover officers, had more latitude to undertake activities that would establish a more ingrained cover, were long gone. Today's undercover officers had to tread this grey line very carefully. The reality, however, was that sometimes minor transgressions of the law were absolutely necessary to maintain their cover and make progress in the case. However murder is not, and has never been, one of those minor transgressions, even if Darby would strenuously argue that he only aided in the death of Jarel Lamar Powel by carrying tools and stepladders.

Darby knew that he was in the shit, and neck deep. On that particular night he had displayed poor judgement and had fallen too deep, too quickly. He should have made his excuses to Shaun and left him to it, whatever the subsequent impact on the trust from within the family. As the night developed, and they drove deeper into the woods, Darby had been hoping that Powell was going to be beaten and left somewhere; this he could have lived with. This he could have reported to his boss and probably, just probably, got away with.

But now he was troubled over the impact on the ongoing case that the team was trying to build against the Dolsen family, but moreover he was worried about his self-preservation. He knew that the truth would come out eventually, but if only he could just prolong it for a few more months.

CHAPTER 14

Have you got everything, Jonny?'

'Everything? I'm travelling there and back in a day, Nic. I'm taking my wallet, my phone, and...' he theatrically patted his front and rear trouser pockets, 'myself. That's it.'

'Okay, fair point.'

Priest was busying himself, but with little or no focus and seemingly in a world of his own.

'Jonny.' No reply. 'Jonny, come and sit down please.' Nicola took his hand as he sat down on the bed next to her. 'I'm sorry I can't come with you today, I really wanted to be there for you.'

'I know, Nic. I'm a bit pissed off that Sawden wouldn't approve a day's compassionate leave for you too, but hey-ho, never mind. It is what it is.'

'Will you call me straight after the service?'

'Yes, of course.'

'Promise?'

'Yes, Nic, I promise,' he said as he gave her a kiss and stood up. 'Right, I need to get on the road.'

'What time is your train?'

'Just after six-thirty.' He looked at his watch. 'And I'm going to miss it at this rate.'

They said their goodbyes and Priest set off for London for his mum's funeral.

Shaun Dolsen had received a call from Davey a couple of hours ago, asking him to meet at The Ink Lounge. The aforementioned business was a tattoo studio owned by Christopher Dolsen, which he had bought from a friend ten years ago. His friend had run into some money troubles after his wife had left him suddenly and cleared out their joint bank account, and Christopher had offered to bail him out; but the price of doing so was his tattoo studio.

Christopher had been interested in tattoos for two decades, and had extensive ink covering most of his torso and both arms. He had even had some work done in this very studio by his friend, so when the opportunity came up to own the studio, he didn't hesitate.

In the years since the studio had built up a good reputation, and an impressive list of customers, including some notable footballers from both the blue and red sides of the city. Christopher had hired two artists from Poland, after a recommendation from another studio owner who didn't have the space in his studio for further artists. Christopher, and The Ink Lounge, didn't regret the decision, and hadn't looked back since.

Whilst the tattoo studio operated as a legitimate business, primarily for Christopher, the building itself served another purpose for the Dolsen family. Above the studio was a two-bedroom flat, not that it had any beds, or any other furniture for that matter. Access to the upstairs flat was gained via a single steel-reinforced door with double deadbolts in three places that secured into a reinforced doorframe. It would take one hell of a battering ram generating some serious energy to take that door down, which was just as well for the Dolsens, due to the large amount of illegal drugs that were always upstairs.

The flat was used for the initial receipt and storing of drugs, primarily cocaine and ecstasy. The tablets were bagged up in batches of five hundred, and the coke was retained in one-kilo bricks. The most trusted soldiers would collect the drugs and disperse them across a number of safe houses, where the coke would be cut using baking powder, and separated into single-gram wraps. By the time their coke hit the streets, it would be no more than forty, perhaps fifty, percent pure. At any one time, the flat probably had five hundred thousand pounds' worth of drugs there, probably with no attempt to conceal them.

When Shaun walked through the door, Jimmy, Davey and Christopher were already there. He checked his watch; he wasn't late, and with neither Davey nor Christopher being known for their punctuality, they were clearly there purposely ahead of him.

'What's this all about then?' asked Shaun, as he took a mug of black coffee from the cafetière on the table top. 'I've got loads of shit I've got to get done today.'

'Tell me about that Yardie that was murdered five or six weeks ago,' asked Jimmy.

'The Yardie? Yeah, fucking good riddance I say. We should seize that opportunity to move on some of their weight.'

'Their weight? Don't be fucking stupid, Shaun. The Yardies are ten times the size we are. We are only tolerated because we stay out of each other's way. No, I'm more interested in your involvement with the murder of this particular Yardie.'

'Involvement? I don't know what the fuck you're talking about, Jimmy.'

'Really? Because that's not what I'm hearing.'

'Little birdie whispering in your ear?' Shaun attempted to make a joke out of it, but Jimmy's motionless face characterised his less than impressed mood. 'You shouldn't be listening to those little birdies, Jimmy, they're full of shit, and don't know the truth about half of the shit they spit out.'

'Oh, I've got a little birdie that I know is telling the truth, and I trust him.'

'Trust him? What, more than me?'

'Right now, yes, Shaun.'

Shaun paused for a while, and quickly assessed his options. Should he continue to front it out and try to call Jimmy's bluff? No, instead he chose to open up, and started to recount most of what Darby had told Davey on the previous night. The elements of the story that Shaun omitted, like the added premeditation of knowing exactly whereabouts in the woods to take the body, were filled in by Davey.

'You stupid fucking idiot.' Jimmy was nothing less than damming in his condemnation of Shaun, and his actions. 'Victoria was murdered as a result of that murder, direct revenge.'

'We don't know that for sure,' argued Shaun, although he knew himself that it was highly probable.

'Be under no fucking illusion, Shaun, I place the blame for Victoria's death squarely at your door.'

There was a moment of silence. In fact, there was generally always a moment of silence when Shaun was backed into a corner. Would he come out fighting and defend his corner, in his usual exuberant way; or just roll over and take it on the chin?

'So what now?' asked Shaun.

'Now? We sit, we reflect, we plan.'

'Plan. For what exactly?'

'Revenge, Shaun. Revenge. You don't think that we are going to let Victoria's death go unavenged, do you? Even if you are to blame for fucking starting this.'

With the temperature in the room finally dialled down a few notches, Shaun took the opportunity to raise something else that Jimmy would be unaware of.

'So...whilst we are all together and in a good mood,' he smiled, a smile that fell somewhere between nervousness and cockiness, 'I've got something else that I want to discuss, and run by you.'

'Okay,' said Jimmy tentatively, 'who else have you killed?'

'Ha ha...no-one. But seriously, what I have done is secured us a pipeline of crack cocaine from a contact of mine in London.'

'A pipeline?' challenged Davey.

'An initial weight of ten kilos per month, rising to twenty-five kilos within six months. I have been liaising with these cockneys for some time, and I went to London a couple of days ago to finalise the deal.'

'Twenty-five fucking kilos, Shaun. That's two million each month.'

'Yes, street value, Davey. Clearly, that's not our cost. Plus, our starting position is only ten kilos per month.'

'Yes, but that's about eight hundred grand. We don't have eight hundred grand lying around to give these fucking cockneys, Shaun.'

'That's not the cost price, I told you. Anyway, we've got that and plenty more, Davey, don't treat me like a fucking numpty.'

'If the cap fits, Shaun.'

Jimmy, who hadn't commented so far on Shaun's admission or Davey's challenges, stood up and walked over towards Shaun.

'Who gave you the authority to make a deal of this size, or of any size to be honest?'

'No-one, Jimmy, I was using my initiative to…' Shaun was stopped mid-sentence by a smack across the head from Jimmy, just like a parent thwacking a rebellious teenager who had just been caught with an e-cigarette in their bedroom.

'I give the orders. I say what we do and when we do it, and this fucking deal is stupid. It's a stupid move, and we're not doing it. We move coke, heroin and ecstasy, we do not move crack. The Yardies move crack across the North West, and we stay clear of it, hence we stay clear of the Yardies. We've got enough fucking problems with the Yardies, let alone adding a full fucking turf war over ten kilos of crack. We're not doing it.'

'We're not doing it?' challenged Shaun, 'why, because you didn't think of it? Because you didn't negotiate it? Because you haven't got the bottle to pull it off?'

Jimmy smacked him again, and Shaun recoiled.

'That will be the last time, Jimmy,' Shaun warned him, but Jimmy stood his ground.

'This family, and you, Jimmy, has lost all of its ambition. Fuck sake, we used to be feared throughout Manchester and the North West. We're subservient to the Yardies, we don't move the same gear that they do, we're afraid to make a move into their market or territories. The family has gone soft. Jimmy, you've gone soft. No-one is looking for new opportunities to grow, to expand, to…make more fucking money. The family has turned into a joke, so yes, I went to London to broker this deal that would deliver a regular pipeline for us, and help us move into a new product, a new market.'

Shaun walked away towards the door, where he paused with his hand on the handle. 'And if the family doesn't want this deal, then fuck you, I'll do it myself.'

As he passed through the exit barriers of the underground station, Priest looked out beyond the arched entrance. The sky was dark and the clouds looked ready to unburden themselves of the tons of rainwater currently being held within. It was no more than a light drizzle when he stepped onto the pavement, and although to his surprise there was actually a taxi waiting at the taxi rank, he chose to undertake the walk that he knew to be about twenty minutes.

The funeral cortege was to set off from his parents' house, and he arrived just in time before the heavens opened. Before he stepped inside he found time to stand on the pavement and take a moment to look at the house; the house where he had been brought up. Aside from his visit two weeks ago when he came back to help with the organisation of the funeral, he hadn't been back to his childhood home for well over ten years.

He looked up at the first-floor facing window that overlooked the road; this had been his bedroom, his view for the best part of the first twenty years of his life. As he swept his head left and right, he noted that nothing had changed, not really. The house directly across the road still had the external wooden faux window shutters, although the garish turquoise of the 1970s had since been replaced with a softer tone of eggshell white. The house on its immediate right, he recalled, would never have settled snow on the roof, even after the heaviest of snowfalls. As a young boy he had sat for hours looking out of his bedroom window and recalled thinking that the roof must have had some special tiles fitted, tiles that had their own heat source, melting the cold snow as soon as the flakes hit the roof. He was a teenager when he found out that the occupiers of the house had a cannabis farm in the loft space, and the heat from both the ceiling lights and the many heat lamps was creating an abnormally high temperature; added to which, they were utilising thick blackout curtains in order to block out the light that was needed twenty-four hours per day. He had been at the window, watching, as the police raided the house one morning and arrested their neighbours. The snow had settled on the roof every winter from that point onwards.

Hydroponics tents, he thought to himself, *that's the difference now, hydroponics tents.*

'Tents? Are you talking to yourself, Jonathan?' It was his Aunt Jayne. He must have been thinking out loud.

'Aunt Jayne, how are you?'

'First sign of senility, you know.'

'What is?'

'You know, talking to yourself.'

'Ah yes, so they say.'

'Listen, dear.' She reached out and took hold of his arm. 'I just wanted to offer my own personal condolences on the loss of Carole. Your mum was a lovely woman. She will be missed, dear.'

'Thank you, Aunt Jayne, that's very nice of you.' Priest gestured towards the front door. 'Shall we go inside?'

They stepped through and closed the front door behind them; the door to the lounge, on their right-hand side, was ajar and Priest looked through. The atmosphere appeared vibrant and high-spirited amongst the twenty-five or so people in there, more fitting to a birthday party or a celebration of sorts than a funeral. He had been spotted.

'Jonathan, Jonathan, Jonathan.' The initial greeting and hug came from Aunt Joan, followed by Aunt Jackie, Aunt Pauline and a further hug from Aunt Jayne despite her having already met him outside less than two minutes ago. The room was filled with aunts, uncles, and cousins, friends of his parents, and the odd one or two people that Priest didn't recognise. Uncles greeted him with exuberant handshakes, and he was offered three cups of tea and a whiskey within five minutes of arriving.

'Where's Dad?' he asked of Aunt Joan.

'I believe he is in the shed, I think he is having a few minutes alone.'

'Okay.' Priest thought about going to see him, then thought better of it. He hadn't spoken to his father for over ten years, and last week's brief visit to sort out the funeral arrangements had done nothing to break the cycle. For all his own pain and sadness, his dad must be hurting right now and he wanted to at least engage, understand and talk it through together, even if he couldn't make the pain disappear. He assured himself that he would look to engage with his father, but perhaps he would leave it until after the funeral service.

The next twenty minutes was a whirlwind, as *Jonathan* was reacquainted with his immediate and extended family, some of whom had travelled considerable distances to pay their respects to Carole. He was engrossed in conversation with Great-uncle Charlie, who had travelled over five hundred and fifty miles from Glenlivet on the borders of Cairngorms National Park, when the funeral cars arrived.

'Jonathan, can you go and fetch your dad?' Aunt Joan's face and tone changed in an instant. 'Your mum has arrived.'

The church service, followed immediately by the committal service at the local crematorium, passed without hitch, and it was at the wake in the Coach and Horses pub that Priest first approached his father, albeit with a mix of Dutch courage and trepidation.

'Can I sit down?' he asked.

'It's a free country.' The response was typical of his father, and Priest almost gave up immediately.

'Can I get you a pint, Dad?' Priest gestured towards the half empty pint of Black Sheep ale on the table, on top of the beer mat.

'I'm alright, thanks. I've got plenty left yet.'

'Okay, no worries, perhaps later. Don't you think that it's about time that we put this behind us now? We should move on; it's been ten years, Dad.'

'Aye, and look where your mother is now.'

'Don't be bloody ridiculous. Mum died from a stroke.' Priest was incensed by his dad's response; yet another inconsiderate and self-regarding remark.

Carole had fallen at home one Saturday morning after her husband had left for work. She had broken her hip. Jonny would visit his parents every Saturday, arriving on the dot at ten o'clock and staying for a couple of hours. On this particular morning, however, he did not come, he had been too busy at work and hadn't found the time to visit. The net result being that his mum had been lying on the floor from just after nine o'clock in the morning until six in the evening when his dad arrived home. As far as his dad was concerned, the fact that he, himself, had been out at work all day was irrelevant to the point at hand; his wife lay in agony, on her own, on the floor, for nine hours because Jonny had failed to call in and see her *as he always did,* and *as he always should.* His dad laid the blame for this squarely at the feet of his son. The weight of blame that Jonny had felt over the last ten years had been incalculable, and had clearly taken its toll.

Carole had made a full, if slow, recovery and had convalesced at home for the following three months, during which his dad had made it quite clear that he didn't want Jonny to visit. But he did visit; he visited when his father was out of the house. His mum had never blamed him once, and never would.

'She's been going steadily downhill since her fall on that day.'

'She's being going steadily downhill? Dad, she's been aging, like all of us. She was seventy-one years old when she died. The fall, on that particular day, had nothing to do with her death.'

'Well, that's what you say.'

'No, Dad, that's what all the doctors said. You know, you were there.' Jonny rose to his feet. 'You're impossible, you really are.' He picked up his drink from the table, and walked away.

After socialising with every aunt, uncle, cousin and family friend in the two adjourning rooms, Priest returned some ninety minutes later to find his father still sitting in the same place, still sitting alone, and probably still cradling the same half-empty pint of Black Sheep ale. Priest felt guilty for walking off; he had to be the bigger man.

He walked over to the table, and as he did, his father looked up at him. 'Do you mind if I sit down again?' He didn't wait for a reply. 'Right, we are both going to start to make more of an effort, Dad. Listen up, I'll going to come back down to London every other month, and I'll bring Nicola for the weekend. We can alternate months, we'll pick you up and you can come and stay with us in Manchester.'

'Come to Manchester?'

'Yes, Dad, you might need your passport to get north of the Watford Gap though; and you might want to look into what inoculations southerners need for a weekend in the north.'

They smiled warmly at each other, as with that brief open exchange their relationship was, well might be, hopefully on the road to recovery finally. It was a shame that it had taken ten years and the tragic death of their wife and mother to bring them together.

CHAPTER 15

Three weeks, almost four, had passed since Priest had returned from London. During this time almost nothing of any significance had occurred; this was certainly true of Priest's investigation into the murders of Jarel Powell and Victoria Dolsen, and the attempted murder of Johannes De Groot.

Shaun Dolsen, on the other hand, had had a relatively busy time, as the first shipment from Tommy Randles had been safely received. This after eventually smoothing the issue with Jimmy, which itself was a challenging and lengthy task.

Shaun had travelled, with Woolhouse again, to London for the exchange. This time the meeting wasn't in a covert, disused warehouse, but a rather more open and public venue. Shaun had been asked to meet Randles at nine a.m. in the car park of the IKEA superstore, in the shadow of the Wembley stadium. Initially surprised at the location and time of the meeting, Shaun had plenty of thinking time on his drive down and realised it was actually quite clever. A meeting, however covert, in the dead of the night would always arouse suspicion from any Tom, Dick, or nosey Plod. Exchanging two holdalls in the IKEA car park full of Saturday shoppers, in a transaction that should take all of twenty seconds, was unlikely to stir anyone's interest. Especially those shoppers trying to wrestle down the back seats of their car in order to fit two Billy bookcases and a large print of the New York skyline into the boot of their hatchback. Once they were safely in and the boot closed, the task was now trying to figure out where little Harry and Ava would sit for the thirty-mile journey home, all whilst the scornful wife looked on in utter amazement; *for God's sake, Stephen, let me do it!*

Despite their two hundred and ten mile drive, Shaun and Woolhouse had been fortunate with their journey and arrived at the IKEA car park just ten minutes before the scheduled meeting time. Randles had seen them pull up, and within thirty seconds one of his men was walking towards their car with a large black canvas holdall. Randles remained in the car and watched from a distance.

Watching him via the door mirror, Woolhouse popped the boot of the BMW just as he arrived. Shaun wasn't as relaxed and composed as Randles and *needed to be in every detail*, so he asked Woolhouse to remain in the car whilst he would alight to meet Randles' man.

Within twenty seconds, holdalls were exchanged and the deal was done. No checks were made on either the money, or the merchandise. Shaun closed the boot on ten kilos of crack cocaine, whilst Randles drove off with a tan leather holdall containing two hundred thousand pounds in rolled up used notes.

Priest had used the normal manpower available on shift to undertake ad hoc surveillance on the Dolsens. He had been watching Jimmy, Davey, and occasionally. However, this was little more than two to three hours each day, and then not all of them at any one time. A request for a more formal, dedicated surveillance team had not been approved by Superintendent Sawden, so Priest had to make do with what he had within his own squad, plus a handful of assigned uniformed officers. It was less surveillance and more occasional 'drive past so we can see that you can see that we are watching you'.

'Just pull in here.'

'Where?'

'Here, on the left.'

Darby looked across and through the side window. 'Antalya Kebabs, really?'

'Yeah, I'm starving. I need some food.'

'There will be a chippy down the road somewhere.'

'Yes, maybe, but I saw this, and now we're here. Are you having anything?'

'No, Shaun. I'll wait in the car.'

'Okay, I'll bring you some doner meat back.'

'Don't; really, don't.' As Shaun exited the car, Darby continued, 'you do know what's in doner meat, don't you?'

Shaun continued walking towards the door. 'I'm not listening.'

Darby found himself shouting through the open window, just so he could make his point before Shaun entered the shop. 'Some elements of beef or turkey, but sausage meat. Sausage meat can contain skeletal muscles, including blood vessels, nerves and fat tissue, basically anything.'

His last few words fell on deaf ears as Shaun had entered the shop, and after placing his order he sat down at one of the heavy plastic tables that, together with the bench either side, was bolted to the floor. No doubt to prevent it from being hoisted in the air and thrown either at the serving staff, or through the front window by some drunken Neanderthal late on a Saturday night.

Expecting *fast food* to be exactly that, fast, Darby grew impatient waiting for Shaun, and decided to leave the car and see exactly what the delay was.

'Are you still waiting?' he asked as he entered the shop.

'Yes, apparently he had to start a new chicken skewer.'

'You're fooling yourself if you think that you're having chicken, Shaun. There's none in that,' Darby said, pointing to the half cooked meat rotating clockwise against a back-burner that didn't look hot enough to melt ice-cream, let alone turn raw meat into salmonella-free, tasty chicken strips.

Darby sat on the bench next to Shaun, both of them with their backs to the window; and that, unknown to them, was to be their mistake.

As the server was about to step out from behind the counter with Shaun's order, he checked his walk and decided to stay put. Neither Shaun nor Darby were looking in his direction, so were unable to benefit from his hesitancy, or the look on his face. Before they knew it, or any had time to react, five men had entered the kebab shop and with military-style precision had wrested control of their arms before placing hoods over their heads. Despite the thrashing about and aimless kicking out, both Shaun and Darby were walked to and bundled into their own car, still sitting on the kerbside with its engine running. The driver's seat had already been occupied and they sped off, closely tailed by an accomplice driving the vehicle within which they had all initially arrived.

Their journey was no more than fifteen minutes, during which time both men had tried and struggled, unsuccessfully, to remove their hoods, and the grip within which they were being held was so tight and constrictive that breathing was becoming laboured, let alone trying to wrestle free.

Both captives were not shy in exploring their extensive range of expletives during the brief journey, but their captors remained silent throughout, and didn't rise to the goading.

They drove into the opening of an underground car park. The car park had closed ten minutes ago; many cars still remained, and no access in or out was permitted after nine o'clock, but for their car the barrier lifted as they approached.

They slowly wound their way down the levels until they reached number five, and pulled up outside of the parking attendant's office. With a more subdued resistance this time, Shaun and Darby were walked inside the office and seated in two chairs. Their hoods were finally removed, and before their eyes could refocus, a single punch landing square on the nose was sufficient to knock them both out for the count.

Darby was the first to regain consciousness; it took him a minute or two for his eyes to focus and his brain to engage. He looked around. He was in a small room that had one door and no windows; to his right-hand side there stood a small table with a microwave and two kettles. Both kettles appeared to be switched on, and currently boiling. There were others in the room, but his mind was drawn to the fact that he was cold, and could feel himself shivering. He looked down and saw that he was naked.

With his eyesight fully focused, and his brain on normal alert now, he noticed Shaun Dolsen in a chair next to him; he had been stripped naked too. He noticed Shaun had his hands and feet tied to the chair. He looked at his, and they were too. He wriggled his wrists and thrashed his legs from side to side, but it made no difference, the bindings stayed firm.

'Who are you, and what do you want?'

Out of the partial darkness that the room provided, a figure stepped forward into the faint light given out by the ceiling bulb.

'Me? Ya not want nor oo I is.' The reply was deep Jamaican patois, and Darby didn't really understand what he had said.

At which point a further three stepped forward into the light.

'Fuck.' Darby knew they were Yardies, and his immediate thought was that neither he nor Shaun were likely to be getting out of this room alive. Darby thought he might have one shot to save his life. It was risky but he chose to go for it. He had absolutely nothing to lose at this point.

'Listen, you don't want to kill me. I'm not who you think I am.' No reply.

'People will know that I am missing, and I'm not talking about the Dolsens. The police will be looking for me.' No reply.

'I'm not part of the Dolsen gang.' No reply.

'Look....I'm a police officer. My name is Officer Simon Darby; I've been undercover within the Dolsen gang for thirteen months. You really don't want the murder of a police officer on your hands.'

'A police officer? You fucking bastard.' Shaun had woken up and had clearly caught the last couple of sentences from Darby. 'I'll fucking kill you.'

'Somehow, I don't think you'll get the chance, Shaun.' Darby's quip could have drawn laughter were it not for the circumstances in which they found themselves.

'You fucking bastard. We trusted you; we let you into our family.'

'That was the point, Shaun.' Darby could see that the continuation of this conversation would serve only to anger their captors, but it was buying them some time and at the very least keeping them alive. However, Darby's self-preservation kicked back in.

'I'm a serving police officer. Look, if you let me go, I'll leave it at that. There won't be any repercussions, I won't be able to identify you.' The Yardies chatted quietly amongst themselves in a deep patois that neither Dolsen nor Darby could decipher.

'Look, you've got Dolsen.' Darby was panicking and chose a final option. 'You've got him. He's the one that killed your guy, not me. I wasn't involved. I'm a police officer, for fuck sake. Let me go, and you can do what you want to him; I won't say anything. I won't.'

'You fucking snake,' Shaun replied, 'you're lower than a fucking snake's belly. Well fuck you.' He looked over to the Yardies. 'And fuck you too.'

After a moment or two the two kettles on the table that had been boiling, and had been dismissed by Darby and largely unseen by Dolsen, clicked off as they reached the desired boiling point.

Shaun's arrogance and misplaced cockiness started to take hold. 'Are we having a brew? I'll have milk and two sugars.' Two of the Yardies looked at each other and smiled, knowing full well that a warm sweet cup of tea was the polar opposite of what their captives were to receive.

'They are not making a brew, Shaun,' advised Darby.

'Fuck off,' came the rather swift and terse retort, 'I'm not fucking talking to you.'

'Suit yourself.'

As the first kettle clicked off, it was picked up by one of the men. He looked towards the far corner of the room, where the silhouette of another man could be seen in the darkness. The bulb above Darby's head barely gave off enough light for the immediate two square metres around him; it certainly didn't do anything to illuminate the far corners of the room. Neither of the captives could see to whom he was looking for approval.

Approval, in whatever form, must have been forthcoming as the man stepped forward with kettle in hand, steam gushing from the spout. He stood over both seated men, and with his other hand rocked his index finger from left to right. Whilst the words were not uttered, he was making his choice – eeny, meeny, miny, moe. His finger stopped moving on Darby, as Dolsen exhaled his relief, accompanied by a sarcastic smirk which didn't go unnoticed.

The Yardie turned his hand, lowered the kettle to a few inches above, and started to pour boiling hot water over Dolsen's right leg. The pain was immediate and excruciating, and Dolsen thrashed his legs sideways to avoid the water, but he did so in vain as the hand controlling the kettle simply adjusted and centralised his aim to maintain the steady flow on his leg.

To Dolsen it felt like minutes. In reality, the kettle had only emptied about the equivalent of one pint of water onto his leg. When the pouring ceased, so did Dolsen's wailing.

'You fucking bastard. You fucking......I'm gonna fucking kill you for this.' That was all he had to say as he refocussed his mind, trying to take back control by blocking out the pain. It wasn't working.

Devoid of all emotion, and with no obvious signs of taking pleasure in the suffering, the man quickly turned the second kettle on Darby. Right leg again. His leg instantly pulled to the side as soon as the first drops of boiling water fell on his skin. Again, a steady hand centred the kettle and kept pace with the trashing of the leg ensuring little or none missed its target.

Once Darby had received his pint, the kettle was placed back on the table and the Yardies allowed themselves a quick exchange of glances. *Fuck me*, Darby thought, *I hope that's all.*

Dolsen was having none of it, brazen as usual. 'Is that all you've got? Fucking pussies. If that's your A-game, then you might as well fuck off home now.'

The look that Darby threw him was priceless; if it could be bottled, it could be marketed as a weapon of mass destruction. The Yardies weren't expecting any glib comments and Dolsen's cockiness, however misplaced, took them by surprise a little. There was only one thing for it....more water.

It is amazing how long it takes to boil an average sized kettle. When you're waiting for your morning brew, it appears to take forever, but in this situation, it seemed far less than a minute before the refilled kettle was boiled and primed for use again.

What I wouldn't give for a fucking power cut right about now, Darby thought to himself.

The guy stepped forward, having picked up the second kettle from the table, and walked over to Dolsen, whereupon he proceeded to empty half of it over his other thigh. Experiencing the pain on the other leg did nothing to prepare him or diminish the pain this time around either, and his contorted face portrayed the discomfort that he was clearly feeling.

After Darby had the same treatment on his other leg, both kettles were refilled and placed back on their stands to re-boil. Three of the captors exited the room, leaving just one to watch over their captives.

The initial intense pain had died down as the body started to fight and take back control. The pain had replaced now by a constant stinging, or numbing sensation, and their legs showed little visible signs of the trauma other than a large red scald mark.

Darby turned his head towards Dolsen, still cognisant of the one remaining guard. 'You've got to rein in that cockiness, Shaun, or they'll just ramp up the pain.'

'Fuck off, copper.'

'Seriously, Shaun? Look with any luck, that's the end of it a bit of pain to scare us off, and they'll release us soon.'

'Release us? You really do live in a parallel universe, don't you? What kind of fucking idiot are you? And how the fuck did we ever get suckered into taking you in?' As a set of rhetorical questions, he wasn't expecting or wanting a reply, and he didn't get one.

'They are not going to release us, they are going to continue to torture us until we die or until they get bored, then they'll dump our bodies somewhere.'

Their brief exchange was interrupted as the other three captors returned to the room, and their hearts sank when they saw two fifteen-litre plastic containers full of water being carried into the room. This coincided with the clicking off of both kettles; boiling point had been reached yet again.

The next hour consisted of the same repetitive, relatively small scale but focused torture; boiling water was poured over their shoulders, their arms, their backs, and their chests. The act itself rarely lasted five to ten seconds, but it was relentless, and their bodies were starting to go into shock.

By now, their bodies had developed partial thickness burns and large blisters had started to appear on both their legs and torso. Limbs were starting to go numb, and it was highly unlikely that any further pain would be felt on their arms and legs.

Two hours in, and one of the captors stepped forward once again, kettle in hand. He stood between Dolsen's legs, his feet having been bound to the chair legs by a short length of coarse rope. A huge grin appeared across his face as he lowered the kettle, and three inches above Dolsen's genitals, he started to pour. Without the protection of a healthy layer of fat, or muscle, the genitals were easily susceptible to injury, discomfort and pain; and God did he feel the pain.

'You animal, you fucking animal. I'm going to fucking kill you…are you fucking listening to me?'

Their captors started to laugh, then the guy holding the kettle made the mistake of lowering his head to the same level as Dolsen's, and laughed in his face. Dolsen's response was to spit in his face. This went down as expected, with the guy reeling back, before hurtling his fist forward and landing a punch against Dolsen's eye. The force was sufficient to knock Dolsen over in the chair, and he fell backwards to the floor, and that's where he was left, at least until Darby had received his own taste of genital pain.

A further round of legs, arms, chest, back, and genitals was pursued by the captors over the following hour, but by the end of the third cycle, and despite the laughs and minor points of enjoyment, they were all getting a little bored. It was clearly now time to step up a gear. There was one area of the body that hadn't been touched yet; their heads.

The prolonged torture had started to take its toll on both Dolsen and Darby. Dolsen's cocky and arrogant swagger had long disappeared, and Darby had been drifting in and out of consciousness as his body was tired of trying desperately to fight back. They hadn't spoken for over an hour, either to each other, or to plead with their captors. The only sounds made remained those of cries of agony, which themselves were more muffled and subdued now.

During bouts of consciousness, Darby had thought it strange that neither he nor Dolsen had been pressed for any information; no details of the gang, no details on the drugs operation, people, distribution, supply lines, and no forced confessions about a dead Yardie found nailed to a tree in the middle of the woods. The Yardies obviously had all the information that was needed, and they were simply extracting their retribution.

Darby summoned all of his inner strength to push the words past his lips. 'No more.' His pleas were almost inaudible. 'No more, please.' His captors didn't respond. Instead one moved to check the readiness of both kettles, once again switched on and boiling away.

In a routine seen two dozen times over the last three hours, both kettles clicked off, and both were picked up simultaneously by two of their captors. In an almost evil and subconscious synchronicity, both sagging heads were lifted and the kettles poured their liquid torture over them.

Dolsen always cropped his hair very short, and the immediacy of the damage was plain to see, whereas Darby's thick mop of dark hair did nothing to lessen the pain, but the damage to his scalp was not as immediately visible. Both their crowns were still visibly steaming long after the water had ceased to pour; and their cries of pain and agony had suddenly now magnified tenfold.

There was only one round to be delivered on their heads, although the kettles were set to boil once again. All of the captors stepped out of the room, leaving no-one to guard them this time; they were going nowhere now.

Darby felt like he was being boiled alive; his breath was becoming shallow and he could feel his heartbeat soften. He had a constant dizzy feeling, his throbbing head was swimming around, and he had to stop himself from falling sideward off the chair. Dolsen, on the other hand, had passed out. Both of them had taken just about as much as their mind and body could handle, and a quick death now would bring some much needed relief and finality to their situation. This was sadistic torture on a prodigious and unprecedented level.

Darby's hopes of either a respite or some finality were dashed when his captors re-entered the room, carrying another fifteen-litre container full of water.

'Enough...enough...enough.' Darby's words were slurred and still barely audible, and they didn't register any interest or acknowledgement with his captors anyway. They proceeded to fill up the two kettles from the container, and huddled together against the far wall...waiting, yet

189

again, for boiling point. Neither Darby, nor a now partially conscious Dolsen, had any idea what lay in store for them, but it couldn't be worse than having boiling water poured over their heads, could it?

Yes, in fact it could. There was little left by way of strength of mind or body, when their heads were tilted back and their eyelids forced open by huge bear-like hands. Boiling water was poured into their open eyes; the natural reaction was to close their eyes and move their head away from the pain, but this was easily mitigated by the firm grasp that their captors had on their heads. There was no wriggling or escaping from this. Both eyes immediately reacted, triggering an inflammatory response as the remaining drops of water dripped onto the eyeball. Almost immediately after the last droplet fell, it all went dark.

With no eyesight remaining, and partial thickness burns to most areas of their limbs and torso, their bodies were shutting down. The once elevated heart rate countering the drop in blood pressure had now slowed to life-threatening levels, and both Darby and Dolsen weren't going to last long.

For most torturers, this would have been enough. This should have been enough. Most captives would have had a bullet through their skull by now, but the Yardies, well, they brought another level of sadism to the table. With the kettles refilled, boiled, and in hand, there was perhaps once final act of merciless and senseless gratification to be had. With the same vice-like grip on their heads, both prisoners received a couple of slaps around the face to ensure they were conscious, then their heads were yanked back and their lower jaws prised open. The kettles tipped, and slowly as a drop reached a trickle, and quickly raced to a gush, the boiling hot water was poured down their throats. The initial feeling, and involuntary response was not far removed from that experienced with 'waterboarding', a form of torture that had been around for hundreds of years, but which had been brought back to notoriety by the American CIA following their alleged use of this torture technique on prisoners. Both Dolsen and Darby found themselves gurgling and spitting water out, but a large volume inevitably passed down their throats.

As if the feeling of simulated drowning wasn't enough, that was secondary to the acute agony brought about from the boiling water itself. Within thirty seconds, their throats started to become inflamed, and they found themselves gasping for breath. The water that had passed through was scalding their stomach, lungs, or both; and the pain…the pain was now simply intolerable.

The entire one and a half litres of boiling water had been poured down their throats, and aside from the odd cough and splutter that prevented some of the consumption, they had pretty much swallowed the lot. Their mouths, down through the trachea and into their lungs and stomach were on fire. As their tracheas narrowed, it started to become difficult, if not almost impossible to draw breath. They both had to be minutes from death.

However long their remaining breath was to last, their captors had one final surprise, although this one would be a welcome relief. From behind their backs, tucked into their belts, two of the Yardies drew knives. These eight-inch zombie knives had one purpose, to cut, and cut deep, and without any hesitation or further showboating, both men had their throats cut from ear to ear.

CHAPTER 16

L ovely morning, this morning, Pete. Just look at the
glorious sun rising in the sky.'

'Aye, it's not bad to look at. But it's a bit nippy, Jeff.
I reckon it's probably cold enough to freeze the balls off a
polar bear.' Jeff laughed.

Jeff Holbrook and Peter O'Brien were railway maintenance workers, and were sixty minutes into an eight-hour
shift on what they were hoping would develop to be a
lovely warm June day. Today's mundane but essential task
was to inspect a five-hundred-metre cable at the side of
the track, half a mile to the east of Gorton railway station.
Having walked from the station to their starting point,
they set about identifying the correct cable, each taking a
ten-metre stretch. The wires inside this particular sheathed
cable supported the railway traffic management system,
specifically the railway signals for the three miles leading
in and out of the station. The cable carried a high voltage,
and would no doubt prove fatal for anyone who touched
the exposed wires.

However unlikely that scenario, Pete, Jeff, and other
men like them, made biennial checks on every metre of the
plastic outer piping to ensure it remained free of damage

and any degradation from exposure to the weather, thus completing their *tick in the box* compliance with the Health and Safety Executive.

Having completed his own ten metres, Jeff advanced ahead of Pete in order to commence inspection of another short stretch. As he walked forward, on the left-hand side just ahead he caught a glimpse of what he thought was a naked body. *Hardly likely*, he thought, although he had experienced this before; just over four years ago he had raised the alarm of *body on the tracks* only to discover upon closer inspection that in fact it was a mannequin. He had been ribbed by his colleagues for weeks after, and had learned a valuable lesson that day about acting in haste.

However, a few paces further forward confirmed what he had initially thought. There wasn't one, but two bodies, and they were definitely not mannequins.

'Pete.'

'Yeah, what's up?'

'Come and see this.'

Pete got up from his kneeling position, and started to advance towards his colleague.

'Fuck!' said Pete, 'that's a bit of an eye-opener.'

'Isn't it just.' Both of them stood still for a few seconds, staring at the bodies. The silence was eventually broken by Jeff as he unclipped his radio from his belt.

'Jeff to base.'

'Go ahead, Jeff,' came the reply.

'Errrr, we've found a couple of bodies. Dead by the look of it, although we haven't checked.'

'What do you mean, bodies?'

'Bodies, as in dead bodies, dead human bodies.' Laughter was heard over the radio.

'Are you playing with mannequins again, Jeff?'

'Bollocks, I'm not joking.'

'Seriously?'

'Yes, seriously. I'm standing here with Pete, looking at two bodies.'

Pete took the radio from Jeff. 'This is Pete. Listen, he's not joking, you had better get someone out here.' He handed the radio back to Jeff.

'Okay, where are you?' said the operator.

'We are at marker sierra delta fourteen.'

'Okay, thanks, Jeff. I'll inform the police. Can you stay there until they arrive with you?'

'Sure. Out.'

It was just after eleven-thirty when Priest arrived on the scene. He had met DS Stephens and DC Simkins in the car park at the railway station, and together they walked along the side of the track, accompanied by a member of Network Rail and a constable from the British Transport Police.

As they rounded the left-hand corner, they could see that the white forensic tent had not yet been erected to cover the bodies, and DC Gilbert was talking to one of the BTP officers.

'Tony, what have we got?'

'Guv, we've got two bodies, both white male and both stripped naked.'

'Okay.'

'They were found this morning around eight-thirty by two railway maintenance workers, Jeff Holbrook and Peter O'Brien. They are back up the road with the transport officers, having a cuppa I think whilst they give their statements.'

195

'Okay, let's have a look what we've got.' Priest moved forward towards the bodies, followed by Stephens and then Simkins.

'Fuck me.' Not Priest's usual reserved reaction to the first viewing of a dead body, or any crime scene, but this was unusual; the bodies were unusual to say the least.

They were the bodies of two males, as DC Gilbert had corrected noted; one lay partially on top of the other, and there had been no attempt to conceal them. Priest looked up the embankment; there was a thick ground covering of brambles all the way up to the top, some twenty metres in vertical height, and a similar distance up the embankment side.

'Could they have been dumped over the top up there, and rolled down to the tracks?' asked Priest.

'That would be my thoughts too, guv,' noted Gilbert, 'the brambles look like they might have been flattened a little with something rolling over them.'

'Yes, I guess.'

'The forensic boys will be able to confirm either way, when they get here, guv; I'm guessing the bodies might have some marks on them.'

'Yes, possibly,' replied Priest, 'although how you would be able to tell, God only knows, because the last thing I can see on their bodies are scratches from bramble bushes.'

'Yes, guv.'

'Tony, can you ensure that we've got a team at the top of the embankment please? Start with the forensic boys, then gather some of the local uniformed officers for a fingertip search one hundred metres either side of this point here.'

'Yes, guv.'

'Oh bollocks; guv, you're going to want to see this a bit closer.' DS Stephens had been taking a closer look at the two bodies whilst Priest had been engaged with DC Gilbert.

'A closer look? Really, Nic?'

'Yes, really.'

It wasn't until Priest was standing directly over both bodies that the full picture of their horrific injuries was laid bare. Both bodies had severe burns on each of their limbs, and their torsos. Their heads were showing signs of burns and scalding to an excessive degree that neither detective had seen the like of before. Both bodies had their throats cut; deep lacerations that extended eight to ten inches, with deep crimson congealed blood covering the edges of the lacerated skin. Their faces were almost unrecognisable; almost.

'You know who these men are, don't you?' Stephens invited Priest to confirm. Priest looked closely.

'No, I don't think so, Nic. Who do you think they are?'

'Take a closer look,' she offered.

'Oh, fuck!' It had taken him a few more seconds. 'It's Shaun Dolsen, and that undercover officer from SOCA......' Priest was searching for his name.

'Darby.'

'That's it, Nic. Darby. Jesus Christ, they are a mess.' Priest stood up and took a couple of steps backwards. 'Well, one thing's for sure, our Yardie/Dolsen gang war has just reached boiling point.'

'I thought it had already,' noted Stephens.

'So...where's Tony?' Priest turned and located him, 'Tony.' Across he came.

'Tony, can you stay on scene with Robert, please? I'm also going to ask Stacey to join you.'

197

'Yes, guv.'

'Can we request that all trains are suspended in and out of Gorton railway station, and any other trains that use this line?'

'Already done, sir,' piped up a uniformed officer from the British Transport Police, 'first thing we did upon hearing that we had bodies on the line.'

'Excellent. Thank you, constable......' The purposeful pause was finally met with a reply as the constable realised the DCI was genuinely asking for his name.

'Harker, sir. Constable Harker.'

'Thank you, Constable Harker. Would you be so kind as to assist my detectives over the course of the next few hours, perhaps acting as liaison between them and your Transport Police colleagues?'

'Yes, sir. Of course. I'll need to clear it with my sergeant first.'

'Yeah, yeah, yeah, yeah.' Priest wasn't looking for an extended conversation.

'Tony, can we seal off the area, probably two hundred metres along the tracks, either side of the bodies? Plus, don't forget about the embankment above, remember?'

'Yes, guv, I've not forgot.'

'Robert, can you liaise with SOCO please, and drop me a text when the forensics boys eventually show up?'

'Guv.'

'It appears pretty obvious that the bodies have been dumped here, so we're really looking for boot prints and tyre markings, I guess; and obviously the usual unique identifiers when they return to the lab.'

'Yes, guv.'

'Oh, and one more thing, text me when Doctor Bell gets here too.'

'I believe he is about thirty minutes away, guv,' Simkins confirmed.

'Good, thank you.'

Priest started to walk off with DS Stephens; he stopped and beckoned DC Gilbert, who dutifully came to his side. 'Oh, one more thing, Tony. These British Transport Police officers are great for nicking pickpockets on station platforms, or any other of the community bobby stuff that they do, but they are not detectives, and not experienced in serious crime investigations, so keep them away from my murder scene, and don't let them trample all over any bloody evidence that we might have.'

Gilbert raised a smile. 'Yes, guv.'

Yet Priest and Stephens started to walk back up the trackside, the very trackside that he had just ordered to be sealed off. No doubt destroying any potential evidence as he plodded along in his size ten shoes, apparently oblivious to the irony.

'I guess we are going to see DI Coker?' Stephens enquired, although fairly confident in her assumption.

'You would be guessing correctly, Nic.'

'Just give me half an hour, Nic, I've got a couple of things to do, then we'll set off to see DI Coker.'

'More important than telling Coker that Darby is dead?'

'As it happens, Nic, yes, right now it is. And as horrible as it sounds, he'll still be dead in thirty minutes' time. Okay?'

'Sure, no problem.'

The CID offices were unusually quiet. DC Gilbert and DC Simkins were on the rail tracks, and DC Wright had been dispatched to join them via a phone call with Priest on their way back to the station. DS Baxter was in Yorkshire for three days, attending one of the College of Policing centres for refresher training on personal safety.

Reading from the personal invitation, DS Baxter had questioned, *why the fuck do I need: a suite of standards and learning resources that are designed to safeguard the safety of police personnel and members of the public, to deal with and avoid where possible conflict situations and to, where necessary, restrain people in the most effective and safest way possible?* DS Stephens had highlighted the point about avoiding possible conflict situations, and left it at that. Baxter had walked off chuntering something about wasting police time, resources and money. Nevertheless, he had dutifully packed for three days and off he went.

Aside from the numerous uniformed officers and non-operational staff, this just left DS Grainger.

'Hi, Pete. What are you working on?' It wasn't meant rhetorically, but Stephens knew exactly what case Grainger was spending most of his time on. She plonked herself on the corner of his desk.

'Oh, hi, Nicola. I'm still juggling my time between the assault outside the Red Lion last Friday night, and the fraudster that swindled a vulnerable old lady out of her life savings.'

'Chalk and cheese, eh?' The puzzled expression on his face illustrated the fact that Grainger didn't understand her comment, so she obliged with an explanation.

'Two completely different types of crime; serious crime, but polar opposites. You know; chalk and cheese.' Her explanation didn't elicit any verbal response either, just an acknowledging awkward smile. 'So how's the victim?'

'A little shocked, as you would expect. I think only just starting to realise the enormity of what happened, and how easy it was. I think her son was more annoyed that she had lost the forty-eight thousand pounds. I think he was banking on the inheritance.'

Stephens smiled. 'I was referring to the victim of the assault outside the Red Lion; but thanks anyway.'

'Oh right. Sorry.'

'It's fine.'

'Yes.'

'Well…?'

'Oh yes. He's still in hospital. He suffered three broken ribs and a fractured eye socket. His vision is still blurry, as is his memory, and with no CCTV covering the area where he was assaulted, we're not making a great deal of progress at the minute.'

'It'll come, Pete. Stick with it.'

'I will, thanks, Nicola. You know me, dogged determination, Nicola, dogged determination.'

'Is your DCI in, constable?' Stephens recognised the voice, and turned to find DI Coker and DS Thomas had just entered the CID squad room.

'Inspector.' She walked towards them. 'DCI Priest is in, yes. Let me just check his availability.'

Somewhat anxiously, Coker advised, 'I need to see him urgently,' and with a far more relaxed tone, Stephens replied, 'and I know he needs to see you also, inspector. As I say, let me check that he is free.'

Having knocked on his door, and entering before she received any reply, Stephens was about to announce their visitor.

'Yes, Nic, I've see them,' he said, his glass panelled office affording him a view of the whole squad room, 'well I guess it saves us a visit to them.'

'Just what I was thinking, guv. Shall I show them in?'

'Sure. Oh, and grab some coffees and a handful of biscuits on the way back, will you?'

She gave him the finger discreetly on her way out of the door.

Everyone had taken a seat, and any opening pleasantries had just about concluded as Stephens re-entered the room with four mugs of coffee but minus the biscuits. On the desk they were placed, and she sat down in the one remaining empty chair.

'We've got something that you should know,' commenced Coker.

'Yes, we too have something that we need to share with you,' replied Priest.

'Okay, but let me start.'

'No,' insisted Priest, 'I think you need to hear what we have to say.'

'This is more important, trust me.' Coker was more insistent; and a quick raise of the eyebrows from Stephens in Priest's direction was enough for him to concede. After all, there was never any real rush to inform someone of a death.

'Forty-eight hours ago, give or take, we received this report from Darby.' From a buff folder he pulled out four pages of crisp white A4 paper, neatly stapled in the top left corner, and briefly waved them in front of his face. For what reason, Priest was unsure, as he hadn't intended to challenge the existence of this very report.

'Darby was supposed to file a written report every week. When he first went undercover thirteen months ago, his reports would be received as regular as clockwork. After a few months, the reports continued, but the frequency and regularity tailed off somewhat. As such, when we received this one a couple of days ago, it wasn't read immediately.'

'Okay; what's so important about this report?'

'This report contains details of the murder of Jarel Lamar Powell, and a confession by Darby as to his involvement in the murder.'

'His what?'

Stephens jumped in for further clarity. 'You mean, Darby knew additional details about the murder that hadn't previously been disclosed in his reports?'

'No, sergeant; I mean Darby has confessed to being there when Powell was murdered, and participating in the event.'

'Participating? Well fuck me. I didn't see that coming,' noted Priest.

'No, me neither.' There was a period of silence when all four quietly reflected on the news. It felt like a few minutes had passed by, but only ten seconds had elapsed when the silence was broken by Coker.

'Clearly the entire case against the Dolsens has now gone tits up; all the information and intel gathered to date will be inadmissible, thirteen months' work wasted.'

'I think that's the least of your worries at the minute,' advised Priest. Coker hadn't heard him, or chose not to, and continued to talk over him.

'Not to mention the embarrassment for SOCA that one of our undercover officers actively participated in a murder.'

'Inspector…'

'I just don't…'

'Inspector. Please.'

'Sorry, what?'

'Look, our news relates to your undercover officer, Darby, too.'

'Oh, right. Has he reached out to your lot in the last day or two?'

'Not really. I'm sorry to inform you that two bodies were discovered at eight-thirty this morning at the side of the rail tracks, half a mile from Gorton railway station. Clearly formal identifications are necessary, and currently underway, however we know that the bodies are that of Shaun Dolsen, and your officer, Simon Darby.'

'Oh shit, you're joking? I mean, you're not joking obviously. Shit. Fuck!'

'I'm sorry. I've got my team at the scene, and by now the police doctor and the forensics boys will be there also.' Priest was initially hesitant about providing further information, but knew that it would come out in due course, and DI Coker would rightly challenge why he wasn't told at the earliest opportunity. 'It looks like both of them were tortured, quite extensively too. I'll share a copy of the autopsy with you when it's completed.'

'Sure, okay.' DI Coker had become sullen; suddenly the probable collapse of the investigation didn't seem important. 'Any initial thoughts as to who might have been involved?'

'Lots of thoughts, but at this stage my best guess would be some kind of revenge attack by the Yardies. That is what I was thinking before you arrived, and now that you've told us about Darby's involvement in the murder of Jarel Powell, it seems more even more plausible.'

'You need to nail these bastards, guv.'

'Agreed, we'll do all we can, inspector.'

'Look.' Coker handed Priest a copy of Darby's last report. 'I'll leave this copy with you.'

'Okay, thank you. I know that it might look like all is lost with your investigation, but I'm sure there are some positive results from some good work, and I'm sure something will come from it.'

'Yes, hopefully.'

'Oh, and I'm sorry about Officer Darby.'

'Thanks. Have you informed his next of kin?'

'No. We can, I mean, we would in due course obviously. Is this something that you would like to do?'

'Yes please, if you don't mind?'

'Of course; I'll leave that with you. Just close the loop and give me a call when it's done.'

'Sure.'

DS Stephens saw DI Coker and DS Thomas out of the building, and returned to the CID room. Priest was standing in front of the murder wall, adding two more names to those of Jarel Lamar Powell and Victoria Dolsen, who were already linked by this vicious gang feud that threatened to engulf the entire city of Manchester and beyond.

The time had rapidly dashed towards six o'clock before everyone arrived back at incident room. It was a hustle of noise and activity as Priest stepped out of his office, and with a single clap of his hands the room fell silent.

'Good afternoon, all.' He checked his watch. 'Well, good evening, almost. I know that most of you are due to knock off shortly, but before we all disappear home, I wanted to conduct a roundup of today's events, plus gather and share any additional information that is relatively new.'

There was some nodding of heads and an overwhelming collective of thoughts aligned to *let's bloody crack on then, because I want to get home.*

'Most of you will be aware,' commenced Priest, 'that two bodies were discovered this morning.' He pointed to two photographs recently placed on the murder wall. 'Shaun Dolsen, one of the Dolsen brothers and key member of one of the most notorious drug gangs across Manchester and the wider North West. The second victim was one of our own boys, PC Simon Darby. Darby was an undercover police officer, working for the Serious Organised Crime Agency. Darby had been undercover for the last thirteen months; his brief was to gather intelligence that would ultimately lead to the arrest and conviction of the key members, plus the dismantling of the Dolsens drug empire. I have some new information to share with you about Shaun Dolsen and PC Darby, courtesy of our colleagues at SOCA, but before I do that, can we have some updates from today?'

Priest scanned the room for the officers to whom the key tasks had been entrusted, and from whom he was now expecting contributions.

'Tony.'

'Yes, guv.'

'Updates from the scene please, from the police doctor and anything from SOCO?'

'Let me start with the doctor, guv. Firstly, he did say that he was going to call you directly, sometime late afternoon or early evening.'

'Okay. Did he allude to anything whilst on site?'

'Nothing that he would commit to, guv. Both bodies were killed elsewhere, and dumped where they were found; and as you saw, both had been subjected to horrific burns injuries received through probably a sustained period of torture.'

'Time of death?'

'He wouldn't be drawn at the scene, apart from to say that it was within the last twenty-four hours. Maybe you'll get more specifics when he calls you, guv.'

'Okay, thanks, Tony. Anything useful from the forensics team?'

'Yes…and no. It was confirmed that the bodies were dumped from the top of the embankment and rolled down through the brambles, resting at the side of the tracks where they were found. As a result of this, we redirected the search teams from the side of the track, up to the top of the embankment. We didn't find anything of interest, having completed a fingertip search over a one-hundred-metre-square grid. There were several different tyre tracks leading up to, and away from, the edge of the embankment, and the SOCO lads got some good images, but no-one is hopeful about these being anything other than run-of-the-mill tyres, found on hundreds of thousands of vehicles.'

'Okay, thanks, Tony. Right, updates from me. DS Stephens and I met with DI Coker earlier this afternoon and obtained some critical information which sheds some light on the murder of our first victim, Jarel Powell, but also fairly comprehensively links the murders of Shaun Dolsen and PC Simon Darby to those of Powell and Victoria Dolsen. I am throwing the attempted murder of Victoria's boyfriend, Johannes De Groot, into the mix too, but I'm certain that he wasn't specifically targeted, and that he was an unlucky victim, having been with Victoria at the time she was gunned down. I have seen a statement from Darby, confirming that both he and Shaun Dolsen were directly responsible for the murder of Jarel Powell. Victoria Dolsen, we are pretty sure, was a direct retaliation by the Yardies;

and our current thinking, which is kind of supported by this new evidence today, is that the Yardies somehow found out who murdered Powell, and that they are responsible for the bodies we found this morning.'

'The undercover cop murdered Powell, guv, is that what you are saying?'

'Yes, I don't have the specifics of who did what and how, but those of you that were at the scene where we found Powell, I'm sure you'll agree it had to be more than one person actively involved. So yes, we now believe that Darby was actively involved in Powell's murder.'

'Fuck me,' exclaimed DC Simkins.

'Yes, thank you for that rather eloquent and articulate contribution, Robert.'

A cheeky smile appeared on the face of DS Stephens; she would enjoy telling Priest a little later, that those were *his* exact words when he found out from DI Coker.

The briefing, albeit it had just about finished, was interrupted as Priest's phone rang. 'Just bear with me a second,' he said as he left the caller on the hook and returned to those in the room, 'right, that's all I wanted to cover, thank you.'

And with that the team started to disperse.

'Sorry, doc, I'm back with you.'

From the other end of the phone, Doctor Bell started to provide Priest with a more detailed update on his findings earlier that day, and Priest kept repeating back what he had heard.

'Both bodies severely burned, possibly by steam or boiling water...... both eyes and throat had been subject to the same burns......alive whilst this was happening... looks like death was, ultimately, due to their throats having been cut. Exsanguination…right, okay. How long before we can expect the autopsy results?'

There followed a period of at least two minutes in which Doctor Bell was justifying why it would take forty-eight hours minimum, as opposed to the *normal* period of twenty-four hours.

'Okay, doc. Understood. If there is anything you can do to speed up the timeline that would be appreciated.' He didn't wait for any response; his finger pressed the red button as soon as he had finished speaking.

'Glad I've caught you, sir,' noted Priest as he entered the open door into Superintendent Sawden's office. He wouldn't normally have got within two feet of the door but Margaret, Sawden's PA, had already left for the evening.

'You haven't caught me, chief inspector. I'm not here.'

'Sir?'

'This is a mirage, I'm already in my car heading home to my wife and a nice chicken jalfrezi that she informs me has been in the slow cooker for six hours.'

The sarcasm clicked with Priest. 'Ah, okay. Well if you're not actually here, then maybe I'll continue talking to the mirage. Perhaps he might be more amenable and give me what I'm looking for.'

Sawden realised that he wasn't going to get out of his office any time soon; he placed his briefcase back on the floor and sat down. 'Right, what do you need?'

'Well, it's connected to the Yardie and Dolsens investigation. You heard about the two bodies that we found this morning, I assume?'

'Yes, I did. I was surprised that you didn't tell me yourself, chief inspector.'

'Yes…sorry…It's been a busy day; and I knew that someone in the station would get word to you. Was it one of my officers?'

'Yes, Detective Sergeant Grainger. I had cause to come to your office whilst you were out, just before you returned probably, and Sergeant Grainger provided a brief precis of this morning's developments.'

'Ah, good. You see, I knew that the team would keep you in the loop; one way or the other.' His tongue-in-cheek comment was met with the faintest of accepting smiles from Sawden. 'Over the course of the day, we have managed to connect both Shaun Dolsen and PC Simon Darby to the murder of Jarel Powell, plus, we are confident that the murders of the aforementioned two were carried out by the Yardies as a direct act of retribution. And when you add in Victoria Dolsen, we have four murders and an attempted murder that we can confidently link to this gang feud across our patch.'

'I'm assuming, chief inspector, that with the loss of SOCA's undercover officer, there is little or no tangible evidence allowing you or DI Coker to make any arrests across these two gangs?'

'I'm fairly confident that the written confession of PC Darby, prior to his death, will be accepted as satisfactory evidence by the Crown Prosecution Service to tie up the murder of Jarel Powell; but as to their own murders and that of Victoria Dolsen, no, sir, we have nothing concrete. As for DI Coker's own investigation, I'm not sure to be honest; hopefully the CPS will find some credibility in Darby, and his submitted reports prior to his last one, and his confession.'

'Okay, so……

'Well, sir, that's why I'm here. I believe we need to start taking a more proactive approach, go on the offensive as it were.'

'I'm all for proactive policing, chief inspector. What did you have in mind? What are you proposing?'

'I want your approval to mount simultaneous raids on the known addresses of eighteen members of either the Dolsen family, or the Yardies. I think it's a little too late for tomorrow morning, so I propose a dawn raid on the day after next.'

'What are you hoping to achieve, chief inspector? I expect you'll find some drugs, more than the average stash of cash one keeps in a house, and with a bit of luck, one or two weapons, but I don't see how these raids are going to help progress your multiple murder investigation.'

'Well...' Priest was cut short; Sawden hadn't quite finished.

'The cost of the operation would be enormous. Eighteen houses, did you say?'

'Yes, sir.'

'Simultaneous raids?'

'Yes, sir, it wouldn't work any other way. Staggering them over the course of the day would be a waste of time. Once we've done the first, word will spread and there will be nothing, or no-one, at the remaining target addresses.'

'Yes, thank you, chief inspector; I was a front line officer for quite a number of years.'

'Yes, sir, sorry.' Priest felt mildly berated.

'You are going to need ten officers at each address, are you not?'

'Ten is protocol, yes, sir, but we could get away with seven. Perhaps eight.'

'Ten officers, eighteen target locations. My maths is telling me that is one hundred and eighty officers.'

'Your maths would be correct, sir. Although this would cap out at just over one hundred and twenty if we reduced the number at each location.'

'Do you really want to risk breaching a target location, undermanned, where you fully expect the occupants to be dangerous and violent, probably with firearms inside?'

'No, sir, obviously….'

'No. You'll need four AFO's at each target address.' Sawden paused for a second, appearing to be quickly doing the maths in his head. 'Seventy-two authorised firearms officers, plus the same number of experienced uniformed officers and detectives. I have to be honest, chief inspector, the cost is prohibitive. Add to which, we don't have seventy-two AFO's, we would need to draw upon surrounding areas, and even then I doubt that would be approved as it would leave other areas seriously depleted, if not operationally ineffective, for several hours.'

'The cost, sir? The cost? These two gangs are responsible not only for four murders in our backyard, but for the distribution of tens of millions of pounds of illegal drugs across the North West. Surely, a proactive and targeted raid across the locations we have identified has a real opportunity to take down these gangs.'

'Take down these gangs? I was under the impression, chief inspector, that your investigation centred on the murder of four individuals?'

'Yes, sir, it does, obviously, but our objectives and those of SOCA appear to be temporarily aligned. I'm confident that we will be able to identify and charge the appropriate gang members with the murders.'

'Appropriate gang members? Let me tell you something, chief inspector, you have zero chance...in fact, less than zero chance of identifying the actual person who killed Dolsen and Darby. Don't get me wrong, bringing these two gangs down and taking several members off the streets for a long stretch will be a good result...but...we, you, are focussed on the murder investigations. SOCA can focus on the drugs element.'

'And SOCA can take the associated cost for these raids?'

'Yes, chief inspector, exactly. The practicalities and cost of the operation that you are proposing are prohibitive. I'm sorry, I cannot authorise such an operation.'

'You can't?'

'No, I cannot. If you want me to take another look tomorrow, you'll need to drastically scale back the operation, by two-thirds probably.'

'When did we make front line operational decisions based on how much it will cost?'

'Always, chief inspector. We have always measured the operational cost against the potential, or probable, upside. And someone of your rank, seniority and experience knows better.'

CHAPTER 17

Two sausages, bacon, two fried eggs, beans, mushrooms and three rounds of toast,' noted Nicola as she peered onto Priest's breakfast plate, 'yep, the English breakfast full monty.'

'Breakfast of champions, Nic, breakfast of champions,' Priest replied, 'oh, and they aren't fried eggs, they are in fact, poached eggs.' He patted his stomach. 'Looking after my weight, see.'

'Yes, well, if you keep eating that several times a week, you'll not be the only one looking at your weight. You'll be under the care of the doctor for high blood pressure, raised cholesterol levels, potential diabetes, high risk of heart disease and stroke, not to mention the additional five stone in weight that you will have added.'

'Really? It's two sausages and a rasher or two of bacon. I wouldn't mind if I was scoffing a pound of lard every other day.'

'Have I put you off your breakfast now?'

'Not bleeding likely.' Priest started to tuck in, but not before he had emptied half a bottle of brown sauce over his plate, much Nicola's disgust.

'Are you going into the station today?' she asked. The question didn't need asking as they shared an online calendar that synchronised their respective work and social diaries, and Nicola could clearly see that Jonny was off all weekend. The joint calendar could always be relied upon, unless that is someone forgot to enter a meeting, social event or shift at work. Then it became redundant and useless; *about as much use as tits on a bull this bloody calendar* as Jonny had once commented when he discovered that Nicola had forgot to enter a Friday night social evening with some girlfriends. This after Priest had booked a surprise dinner at Luigi's, where there was a four-week waiting list for a reservation.

'No, babe, I'm off all weekend. Robert is duty officer all weekend, so barring any major incident, the weekend is ours. What did you want to do?'

Before she could answer, Priest's mobile phone came to life, *but of course it bloody did.* The phone was a few metres away on the kitchen sideboard, so Nicola had a few seconds to listen to the ringtone.

'Pharrell Williams' 'Happy'? What happened to Wagner's 'Ride of the Valkyries'?'

'You've got to move with the times, babe, you know, keep up with the hipsters.' Nicola started to laugh.

'You've had the Wagner classical ringtone for as long as I've known you. Add to which, the Pharrell song was released in 2013, which puts you about five years behind the *hipsters.*'

'I said that you need to move with the times, babe, never committed to being right up there with the *youth.*' The phone was answered just before it rang off.

'Priest…Hi, you okay?…Okay…yes,' looking at his wristwatch, 'that should be okay…no, I'm not going to the station today, let's meet…yes, the Spread Eagle will be fine. About noon?…See you there.'

Any hopes that Nicola had of some time together that afternoon had seemingly dissipated in the space of a thirty-second phone call.

'Well?'

'DI Coker. He wants to meet and chat through a couple of things.'

'Can't it wait until Monday, Jonny?'

'Well, he seemed quite agitated, and well, insistent.'

'Insistent? It's Saturday, and you're a DCI for fuck sake. Just say no.' Nicola was surprised by her outburst, and immediately quick to silently admonish herself. She wasn't whiter than white when came to swearing but on this occasion, she herself saw no reason for her profanity. She had been living with Jonny Priest for too long, that was for sure.

'Sorry.'

'It's fine,' Priest laughed, in between swallowing the remains of his final sausage, 'look, I'll be out about between eleven-forty and, well, probably a couple of hours, then I'll be back. Okay?'

'Sure, but don't come back pissed, Jonny.'

'Pissed? I'm going in the car, babe...that is...unless you want to drop me in town?' Nicola's lack of response, or any form of acknowledgement to his question, was all the confirmation he needed.

'I thought that we might go to the cinema later this afternoon, perhaps around four-ish.'

'Cinema?' Jonny's monotonic answer was as telling as Nicola's earlier silence.

'Well, we don't have to. If you...'

'No, the cinema sounds good, babe. Good movie, big box of popcorn and some back row action. What do you fancy watching?'

'There will be no *back row action*, you're not sixteen anymore, even though your brain probably tells your body that you are. There is a new Ryan Reynolds movie out. Some of the girls at the station have seen it, it's meant to be really good.'

'Okay. Ryan Reynolds it is. Text me the start time, and I'll make sure that I'm back in good time. See you later.' And with that, he was off.

Priest closed the door behind him. Immediately Nicola reached for the iPad to check the screening time of the movie, whereas Jonny was walking towards his car thinking, *who the fuck is Ryan Reynolds?*

It took Priest about thirty minutes to reach the Spread Eagle. Truth be told, it took him fifteen minutes to reach the car park that was within two minutes' walk of the pub, but it took a further quarter of an hour to park his car. During his fifteen minutes in the car park he drove around several times, chuntered *fucking Saturday shoppers* at least four times, and twice waited for a car to pull out of a parking space only for another car to steam in ahead of him and steal his parking spot. *Fucking Saturday shoppers.* These were the times when he wished he wasn't a senior police officer, and had a little perceived latitude to beat the living daylights out of some of these obnoxious and ignorant motorists.

Arriving ten minutes late, Priest was not surprised to find DI Coker already inside the Spread Eagle and ensconced in a nice snug booth area towards the right of the entrance, cradling a pint.

Priest caught his eye, and with the universally recognised hand gesture enquired if he wanted another drink. With confirmation that he did, Priest dutifully ordered.

He placed both drinks on the table and sat across from Coker.

'I don't even know your name.'

'What do you mean? It's Coker.'

'It's Saturday for fuck sake, and we're off duty; well I am, anyway. I'm not calling you DI Coker.'

'Fair point, it's Andrew. And you....Jonathan, I believe?'

'DCI Priest to you, you cheeky bugger.' The immediate smile confirmed he wsas joking. 'Jonny will do on a weekend.'

They both took a couple of slugs of beer, whistles wet and ready for some dialogue.

'So, how can I help you? Is this personal, or are we talking shop?'

'We are talking shop.'

'Okay, go on.'

'Would it be correct to assume that you are going to investigate the murders of Shaun Dolsen and PC Simon Darby?'

'Yes, of course. I've opened a murder enquiry into both Dolsen and Darby. We know that the murders are clearly linked to the Jarel Powell and Victoria Dolsen murders, plus the attempted murder of her boyfriend; but if as expected these are Yardie revenge killings, we are unlikely to make much progress.'

'So, you're giving up then?'

'No, that's not what I said. We have no witnesses, and I'm less than hopeful about any forensics. Look, Andrew, it appears to me that through your tenure with SOCA you've probably got more knowledge and experience than I have in relation to gang culture, gang violence and the likelihood of being able to tie a specific crime to a specific individual without any witnesses or forensics.'

'Yes, I know, but…'

'But…you feel a sense of responsibility and guilt over Simon Darby's death, don't you?' Coker didn't need to respond, his answer was written all over his face.

'What are SOCA's lines of enquiry at present? Clearly we need to be coordinated on this if you are still pursuing the Dolsens, and are continuing with your active investigation.'

'Agreed,' replied Coker, 'our investigation will continue until we are told otherwise. We've got too much invested in this to walk away now.'

'Agreed. So, what movement have you seen over the past few weeks, or even days?'

'Well, Jimmy Dolsen has clearly been rocked by the death of both Victoria and Shaun. Add to which, he's recently discovered that he has had an undercover cop working within his inner circle for the last eighteen months. So he appears to have retrenched and effectively pulled down the metaphorical shutters.'

'How…' Priest stopped himself asking the question. The murders of both Dolsen and Darby had been extensively covered in the media, and once Darby's occupation had been discovered, this element appeared to be the leading edge of the story. All Jimmy had to do was pick up a local paper to read about the *brutal murder of PC Simon Darby*, although the media were clearly ignorant of his undercover role. It was fairly easy for Jimmy to join the dots.

'We've been keeping tabs on Jimmy, and to be honest he's rarely left his house over the last few weeks.'

'Well, as reassuring at that might be, we both know he has an army of soldiers on the streets still continuing to help run his distribution and supply. He can sit in his house all fucking year and his business will still roll on, and I guess that is, and always has been, your challenge; catching Jimmy with his hands dirty.'

'Correct. As I've said before, through PC Darby's information we have always had enough evidence to get all of the gang put behind bars for two or three years, probably...but...it was never about getting them off the streets for a two-stretch, it was about completely dismantling their operation and securing jail terms that would see them spend the majority, if not all, of their remaining lives behind bars.'

'What movement have you seen within the Yardies?'

'Very little, if I'm honest. Our operation has always been about the Dolsen gang. What our intelligence tells us is that the Yardies are no doubt experiencing some infighting; they're disjointed and lacking some short-term focus. This will be corrected in the near future as someone steps up and challenges for the leadership role. Rumours are that the new leader is likely to be Ezekiel Johnson, the guy from the aborted abduction a couple of months ago.'

'And then...' Priest asked.

'And then, he will either gain the support of the soldiers, or there's likely to be some kind of leadership battle, which might result in a death or two.'

'Hmmm, every cloud and all that...' There was an inappropriate but mutually accepted chuckle from both of them.

'Tell me about the aftermath of Darby's confession, and any further shockwaves felt through SOCA.'

'Well, it would be fair to say that the whole unit is still in shock over PC Darby's death.'

Priest thought it slightly strange that even now Darby was not referred to by his first name, Simon. For sure Coker was the senior officer, and in fact was the boss of his boss, but it showed a lack of empathy and perhaps an acknowledgement that Coker didn't really get to know his officers, or form any type of personal or informal relationship.

'Our super is quote, *really disappointed,* unquote, and has intimated that this is likely to have a potentially wide-ranging impact over the coming months, and probably years to come.'

'Really, how so?'

'Well, I can see the number of undercover operations being cut back dramatically, all over the country. We'll no doubt become so PC and risk averse that most undercover operations will become unviable. Checks on this or that, hurdles to overcome, hoops to jump through and so many restrictions that we simply won't be able to run an effective undercover operation.'

'I get the frustration, I do, and yes I agree this is bound to limit the scope of what you are able to achieve as an undercover unit. But…'

'But…?'

'But PC Darby was, by any stretch of the imagination, acting well outside of his operating parameters. I mean, what the fuck possessed him to participate in a murder, even if he believed it was necessary to maintain his cover? It might have been an isolated incident, Andrew, perhaps from a single rogue officer; but a back to basics review of undercover operating parameters, and oversight protection and governance, sounds like a wise if not necessary move.'

'Yes, perhaps.'

'There's no perhaps about it.'

Both of them downed the balance of their beer and Coker stood up, picked up the empty glasses and made his way to the bar. He placed his order with the barmaid, then returned to the table.

'Also, I heard yesterday that PC Darby's death is going to be used as a case study at the annual Police Superintendents Association conference in a few months' time. Apparently my boss is presenting a two-hour workshop on *the psychological support available for undercover officers and covert operatives.*'

'Covert operatives? We are police officers, we're hardly James bloody Bond.'

'I know.'

'Sounds fucking riveting,' noted Priest, 'no disrespect meant.' His brazen comment was simultaneously balanced with a smile affirming his witticism.

'Yeah, I know what you mean, I'm glad I'm not attending the conference, that's for sure.'

Whilst the two had been chatting, the barmaid had delivered the beers to their table, and was suitably rewarded by Coker with the change from his ten pound note. At over four pounds a pint, it did cause the barmaid to openly verbalise her feigned excitement at the thought of spending her one pound seventy-two pence.

Priest decided to open up a little to Coker. 'I proposed a series of wide-scale raids across known locations of both the Yardies and the Dolsens.'

Coker looked surprised.

'Don't worry, I would have looped you in, but as it happens the raids were not approved by my super.'

'Really, why?'

'I proposed targeting eighteen locations simultaneously.'

'Eighteen! Jesus Christ, that's a hell of an operation.'

'Yes I know. The problem was that we didn't have sufficient AFO's to support that operation.'

'Yeah, I can see that. Occupants known to be violent and likely to have weapons on site; you'll have needed plenty of AFO's at each location, times eighteen, bloody hell. Do we have that many AFO's across the North West?'

'Yeah, well that's where the plan fell down, or at least it was one reason why it was rejected. We could have actually got the numbers we needed by drawing on surrounding forces, well probably, but the operation never got off the ground because of cost.'

'Cost?'

'Yeah, good old fashioned fucking dollar bills. On balance of probability, the risk and cost far outweighed the rewards.'

'I bet that stung a bit?'

'Yeah, too right. Anyway, perhaps I'll look to revisit it in a few months if we haven't made any significant breakthrough by then.'

'Do you think your super will be more amenable then?'

'Probably not, to be honest, I might have to scale down the operation. I might have to focus on one gang or the other. We either go hell for leather on the Yardies, or the Dolsens.'

'What's your preference?'

'Good question. I have a feeling that taking the Yardies out of action would have a bigger impact across the whole of the North West; and I'm thinking, and hoping, that we are more likely to find drugs, cash and weapons at their targeted locations, than we are at the Dolsens. Having said that, dismantling the Dolsens' infrastructure would be a big coup too. Either way, I have to be mindful that my team and I are trying to investigate several murders, and this needs to be our priority. Perhaps we should leave SOCA to torpedo the bows of the drug gangs.'

There was a moment of uncomfortable silence as though both of them realised that they had nothing left to talk about. The period of silence was filled with awkward smiles and plenty of occasions where their respective pint glasses were raised to their mouths in order to avoid conversation. Eventually though, enough was enough.

'Right, I've got to go. I've got to meet Nic, apparently we are spending the afternoon with Ryan Reynolds.'

'Ryan Reynolds, the Hollywood actor?'

'Yes, the very same. Apparently we have a timed slot, and I've been told that I cannot be late.'

'Wow, my wife is mad for Ryan Reynolds. Where are you meeting him? I didn't know he was in the UK. Does he have a premiere this weekend? How did you manage to...'

Coker smiled. Priest smiled.

'Ryan Reynolds, timed slot; you're off to the cinema, aren't you?

'See you soon, Andrew, no doubt.'

CHAPTER 18

Having made it in time for the six a.m. train out of London Euston, DI Coker was expecting to be at Manchester Piccadilly just before eight-thirty. He hadn't reserved a seat, as he had not expected the early train to be busy. He was wrong. Nevertheless, he found a vacant aisle seat with a table that he was to share with three other travellers for the next couple of hours.

Unfortunately even though the time was still before nine a.m. Lady Luck was not to be on his side, and the day was about to take a bite-sized chunk from his schedule.

The train had stopped a few miles short of Macclesfield, and had been stationary for an hour. There had been scant updates from the train driver via the PA system, although he had apologised two or three times for the delay, and reminded everyone that the buffet carriage was fully stocked with refreshments.

'I bet someone has jumped,' noted the elderly woman sitting directly across from Coker. He ignored her.

'You know,' she prodded at his resting arm, 'someone has probably jumped off a bridge, or into the path of a moving train.'

'No, I don't think so. I'm sure it's just some faulty signals up the track. We'll be off again soon no doubt.'

'The train drivers always call it a police incident,' said the elderly gentleman sitting across from him, and next to the woman. Coker hadn't managed to ascertain whether the elderly man and woman were husband and wife, or travelling companions, or simply strangers. They were already in their seats when Coker took his, and as far as he could recall they hadn't spoken one word to each other throughout the journey. *Probably married then.*

'I'm sorry.'

'The train driver, whenever there is a suicide on the tracks, the driver always mentions it in his updates, as a *police incident.*' This was entirely plausible, thought Coker, although he had never been on a train that had been delayed due to a *police incident.*

'Ladies and gentlemen.' The PA system crackled, and the train driver was commencing yet another update. 'Continued apologies for the delay; this is due to a police incident ahead of us.' The old man raised his eyebrows. 'And we should be moving again in the next twenty to thirty minutes. Once again, please accept our apologies for the delay, and feel free to avail yourself of the tea, coffee, and various breakfast items that can be purchased in our buffet car, carriage F.'

'You were both right,' acknowledged Coker, 'it sounds like potentially it could be a suicide.'

'Horrible business,' said the woman, 'have you ever seen a jumper?'

'Err, no, I haven't, and I'm not sure that I would want to either,' confirmed Coker.

'These Class 390 Pendolino trains,' piped up the gentleman; they were now like a double act, tag-teaming on the story, 'they travel at one hundred and ten miles per hour.'

'Is that right?' Coker feigned his interest.

'That'll make a right mess of you, if you step out in front of that.'

'Yes, I've no doubt.'

'Add to which,' it was the woman's turn again, 'these lines are electrified, so the jumper could jump off a bridge, down to the tracks and get electrocuted, then get hit by the train.'

'Okay, well let's hope that it's not that serious, hey?' Coker looked at his watch; nine a.m. Coker had assumed, hoped, that the conversation had come to a natural end, but just as the woman opened her mouth to re-engage, he was saved by an incoming call on his mobile. A withheld number.

'DI Coker.' The phone was answered with the same degree of crispness and brevity that was obviously common across many, if not all detectives.

'Inspector, my name is Greaves, I'm calling from the Crown Prosecution Service.'

'Mr Greaves, yes, bear with me a second please.' Coker rose from his seat and walked to the rear of the carriage and into the enclosed vestibule area. This was potentially, and probably, a conversation that he didn't want the entire train carriage overhearing.

'Sorry about that. Greaves, did you say?'

'Yes, John Greaves, from the CPS.'

'I assume this is about Jimmy Dolsen and the extended family?'

229

'It is, correct.'

'Okay, go on.'

'Well, after review and due consideration we, I mean, the CPS, have decided that we will not be proceeding with the case. I'm afraid that we cannot support any charges brought against James Dolsen or the rest of the potential defendants referenced within the document...' He seemed to scramble for the reference whilst obviously flicking through numerous papers. 'Yes, document NW475-CVA.'

Coker was less than impressed, but took a moment to absorb and reflect on the information, prior to formulating his response. 'You have got to be fucking joking?' Clearly he hadn't taken long enough to reflect.

'I'm sorry.' The young caller from the CPS had clearly not expected that response.

'Why? Tell me why for God's sake, why?'

'Well, to be honest, inspector, PC Darby's participation in the murder of Jarel Leroy Powell has simply discredited him too much, to the point where any and all evidence gathered and submissions received, are simply tainted to the extent of being unusable. He has zero credibility, alive or dead. I'm sorry.'

It was a brunt and brutal assessment, and one, if Coker was honest with himself, that he had expected. That being said, he wasn't about to accept this without a fight.

Greaves continued, 'PC Darby's evidence isn't inadmissible, by any means. From what we have seen, the evidence gathered appears to be fairly strong and could have, potentially, resulted in James Dolsen and the rest of them being given custodial sentences.'

'But?'

'Yes, inspector, but...the defence counsel would have argued that all this evidence was gathered by a man who was willing to go to any means to ensnare their clients, and that, by his own admission, this would extend to participating in murder.'

'This is not acceptable,' noted an incensed Coker, 'this is not how eighteen months of work is going to end. These bastards are responsible for importing and distributing millions of pounds of Class A drugs, and are indirectly responsible for the death of PC Darby.' The last statement was a bit of a stretch, having considered the facts at hand.

'I'm sorry, but that's our decision.'

Coker was now grasping at straws. 'Can I ask, Mr Greaves, what job do you have at the CPS?'

'Sorry, what do you mean?'

'Exactly as I said; what is your job, your role, your position at the CPS?'

'Well, I'm a paralegal officer, in the Complex Casework Unit.'

'A paralegal?'

'A paralegal officer, correct.'

'For fuck sake, one of the most important cases that might cross the desk of the CPS in a decade, and I've got a fucking administrator telling me what's what.'

'Err...' John Greaves was clearly looking to correct Inspector Coker on his understanding of exactly what a paralegal actually did, but he never got the chance.

'I'm not having this, I need to speak to the Chief Crown Prosecutor.'

'I'm sure you do, inspector, but that isn't a call that I can connect you for.'

'I kind of guessed that. Is that because she is the boss of the boss of the boss that bosses your boss?' No reply. Coker ended the call. Just as he did, the train started to move again, to cheers that could be heard either side of him in the carriages.

He dialled another number.

'Guv, it's DI Coker.' He spent the next two minutes replaying the conversation with the CPS to his superintendent, although the two tunnels through which the train passed did little to support a fluidity of the conversation.

'Look,' said the superintendent, 'I'm only getting every other word. Why don't you call in and see me as soon as you arrive.'

As Coker exited the train station, he retrieved his phone from his jacket pocket. 'Can I speak to the Chief Crown Prosecutor, Sandra McHale, please?'

'Who's calling?'

'Detective Inspector Coker from SOCA.'

'Just putting you through, inspector.' Coker held his breath; this sounded hopeful.

'Hello, Chief Crown Prosecutor's office.'

'Hello, can I speak to the Chief Crown Prosecutor please?'

'Sorry, I'm afraid that she is in a meeting, and will be for the next couple of hours. Would you like to leave a message?'

'No thank you.'

When DI Coker arrived at the office of his superintendent, he was met with the news that he, or his PA at least, had been busy and had secured a call with Sandra McHale for one o'clock, later that afternoon. After thanking the superintendent for setting up the call, and having completed his briefing that had been interrupted by the loss of signal on the moving train, Coker returned to his office.

He busied himself doing pretty much nothing, except checking the clock every ten minutes. There was little that he could, or wanted to do; the importance of this call couldn't be overstated. He was hoping that Ms McHale didn't cancel on them.

The time finally arrived, and DI Coker entered the outer office.

'He's waiting for you,' announced the PA. Coker entered the office and took a seat as gestured by the superintendent.

They waited a while, in silence. Coker opened his mouth, about to break the silence, when the phone rang.

'I have the Chief Crown Prosecutor on the line for you.'

'Thank you, Charlotte.'

'Sandra, how are you? It's been a while. Yes, yes. Family keeping well? Yes, yes.' He looked up at Coker. 'Let me put you on hands-free speaker as I have my DI here with me.' He did so, and Coker could now hear her voice.

'DI Coker?'

'Yes, ma'am.'

'You don't need to call me ma'am, Sandra will do. Right, one of my staff tells me that you are unhappy with our decision not to proceed with the prosecution of James Dolsen and a number of his associates, correct?'

'Yes, that's correct. I…' Coker was cut short.

'I don't need any further explanations or elaborations, inspector. I have read the file in detail twice, and this call, courtesy of your superintendent, is simply for me to reiterate the position of the CPS, and the rationale behind our decision.'

The next three to four minutes were spent in silence from the perspective of the two police officers. The Chief Crown Prosecutor backed up and reiterated, verbatim at times, what her colleague had told Coker earlier that morning.

'These conversations normally end with me advising you to go away and obtain better evidence that will provide the CPS with a higher probability of achieving a conviction. But that isn't this conversation; your evidence is good, really good. First-hand account from a serving police officer, it doesn't get much better than that,' she paused, 'well, unless you have audio and video evidence. Anyway... No, this conversation centres solely on the fact that I cannot, and will not, stand up in court and defend or justify the honesty, integrity and credibility of PC Simon Darby.'

And that was that.

CHAPTER 19

Six weeks had motored by in a flash since DI Coker had received the news from the CPS, and in that period very little activity had been undertaken in the Dolsen investigation.

Coker had, however, been making quite a nuisance of himself at the CPS. Several phone calls to different people had resulted in nothing, emails to a wide range of people had received no responses, and on a couple of occasions Coker had visited the CPS offices, but without an appointment he didn't really get past the reception area, let alone in to see the Chief Crown Prosecutor.

Coker was in the squad office perched on the edge of Sergeant Thomas's desk chatting, when his office phone rang. He ignored it and it rang off.

Several of the phones rang simultaneously in the office, and one was picked up by Constable Woolfson. 'Boss, it's a message from upstairs. The super wants to see you in his office.'

'Okay, thanks.'

Wandering up the back stairs to the fifth floor, Coker was running through in his mind how he thought the pending conversation would go. He would be told officially that the books should be closed on the Dolsen case, he would no doubt be given a bollocking for harassing the CPS over the last few weeks, and probably be given a new case to get his teeth into; if he was lucky.

'In you go, inspector,' uttered the PA as he closed the outer door behind him, 'he's waiting for you.'

'Thank you.'

'Inspector Coker, come in, come in.'

'Yes, sir.' Coker took a seat, despite not being asked or encouraged to do so.

'Right, I'll get straight to the point. I've just received a call from Sandra McHale, you know, the Chief Crown…'

'The Chief Crown Prosecutor, yes, sir, I know who she is.'

'Indeed. Well, she called to say that you have been making rather a nuisance of yourself in the last few weeks.'

'Sir…' He was cut short with a waft of the hand.

'Never mind that, means justifying the ends and all that.' Now Coker hadn't a clue what he was talking about; was he getting a reprimand or not?

'Anyway, the CPS took the opportunity to relook at the case, and Ms McHale, I'm advised, looked at it personally. She is satisfied that the case will pass the evidential stage, specifically that there is enough evidence to provide a realistic prospect of a conviction against each defendant on each charge. But that was never the issue, as you know, the CPS have always maintained that the evidence gathered was strong.'

'Agreed,' confirmed Coker, 'so what has changed then?'

'She advised that due consideration had been given as to whether the evidence can be used, and will not be discredited along with PC Darby. The CPS have been weighing up what the defence counsel's case may be, and the potential impact on the prosecution.'

'Well, it's obvious isn't it? Nothing has changed.'

'Correct, it's the same issue, inspector. The defence counsel, even in the face of almost irrefutable evidence, will focus on PC Darby's involvement in the murder of Jarel Powel, and will look to discredit both him and the evidence obtained by him. And this, as you know, was the sole reason why the CPS decided originally not to proceed.'

'Again, agreed. So what was the point of the phone call then?'

'Well, Ms McHale has been reading the reports that were submitted by PC Darby over the period of twelve or so months; and if the judge will allow them into evidence, and if…and it's a bloody big if…the jury can see past the murder involvement, then it's worth a shot apparently.'

'Excellent, bloody hell, sir, that's a bit of a U-turn don't you think?'

'Well, it's pretty much unprecedented. With all the information to hand, I've certainly never heard of the CPS taking a risk like this; they tend to only want to progress with cases that you would bet your mortgage on.'

A couple of seconds of silence and reflection followed. 'Right, inspector, hop to it, I'm guessing that you've probably got lots to be getting on with now.'

'Yes, sir.'

Coker had gathered his small team; himself, Sergeant Thomas, and Constables Winstanley, Woolfson and Bowen. A round of cheers and hi-fives followed the news conveyed by Coker.

'We've got lots of work to do. I want them all in custody within seventy-two hours.'

Over the next six hours details were confirmed, additional resource seconded and raids planned to bring in Jimmy, Davey, and Christopher, plus eight other members of the gang who were clearly implicated in PC Darby's evidence, including senior members Lambert, Kiveton and Woolhouse.

Coker had decided a low-key approach was preferable with no firearms units required, no simultaneous dawn raids; they were simply to identify the location of each of their targets and send two or three officers to facilitate the arrest.

As the time approached ten in the evening, everything was set for tomorrow. Coker had just one thing left to do.

'DCI Priest, it's DI Coker.'

'It's rather late, inspector.' Priest checked his watch. 'What can I do for you?'

'Nothing. Just a courtesy call to let you know that we are picking up Jimmy and ten others tomorrow.'

'Tomorrow? Okay, how? Why?'

'The CPS did a U-turn and decided to proceed with the case.'

'Bloody hell, that's a result. How did you manage that?'

'To be honest, I'm not entirely sure, but nevertheless we are planning to take them into custody tomorrow.'

'Brilliant, well done. Listen, keep me in the loop, will you?'

'Yeah, of course.' Coker silenced his mobile phone, returned it to his pocket and set off home.

CHAPTER 20

Daylight had broken just before seven a.m. DI Coker had enjoyed the thirty-five-minute journey to work, not just because he was anticipating a successful and rewarding day, but, well, the journey was quite easy and stress-free. There was very little traffic on the roads, it being Saturday morning, and with his direction of travel mainly northerly, he had the rising sun to his right most of the way. The vibrant ochre would no doubt have been far more beautiful as it slowly made an appearance over the horizon across the moors, but the industrial backdrop of Manchester was where he was travelling this morning, and that would do just fine.

Occasionally averting his eyes from the road, he felt the vibrancy of the early morning sun fill him with an inexplicable sense of joy, enthusiasm and emotional energy. Despite being inside his car with the windows closed, he took an exaggerated inhale of breath, and exhaled slowly. He was calm, he was relaxed, he was focussed. Today was going to be a good day.

DI Coker had chosen to be part of the team that arrested Jimmy Dolsen; of course he had. In line with his low-key approach, he had two uniformed officers with him. Sergeant Thomas had been tasked with picking up Davey Dolsen, and the balance of his small team, Constables Winstanley, Woolfson and Bowen were to focus on Christopher and two other senior members of the gang. With each team comprising just three officers, and a small mobile group that could be called upon if necessary, the team received a final briefing and were wished good luck by DI Coker.

As the clocked turned nine-thirty, the job was done. Ten of the eleven targets had been apprehended; and all had been at the targeted addresses, with the exception of Christopher. Having tried his home initially, Constable Winstanley had diverted his team to the tattoo studio that Christopher was known to frequent on a Saturday morning. It was a bit early, but the gamble paid off and he was arrested, face down on the laminate wooden floor of the shop.

PC Darby's reports submitted over the last twelve-month period had provided a wealth of information, not only on the active gang members, where they lived, and the vehicles they drove; but also details of all of the properties that the Dolsens owned, either legitimately, or in some cases 'off the books'.

DI Coker had amassed a list of thirty-seven residential addresses, the Ink Lounge tattoo shop, three nightclubs: Zanzibar, The Avenue and the Adelphi; a list of eight public houses and a string of lock-up garages along the length of Oldham Road. Unsurprisingly, very few of the properties were actually registered under the Dolsen family name, and previous searches on the Land Registry and other databases discovered a small number of shell companies, but in the main, properties and businesses had been registered in the names of numerous individuals. None of them were immediately identifiable as immediate or extended members of the gang, but over a period of several months, and with the placement of some tactical questions, PC Darby had managed to link the registered owners to the Dolsen family. Some associations were tenuous in the extreme; for example, if you didn't know that Jimmy Dolsen had told Bernard Stoker, some twelve years ago, that his wife was cheating on him, then you wouldn't know that in return for this information, and 'favour' bestowed, Jimmy had asked Bernard to become the registered owner of the Fox and Hounds in Cheetham Hill. Bernard frequented the pub occasionally, but he certainly didn't get involved in the day-to-day management, let alone make any decisions.

Coker was fairly confident that, under the Proceeds of Crime Act, every one of those properties could and would be confiscated under the principal legislation of money laundering. But that was months down the line, for now the focus was getting Jimmy Dolsen and the others back to the station and placed in holding cells.

As Coker was transporting Jimmy Dolsen back to one of five police stations that had been selected to hold the eleven men, he received a call from Constable Winstanley.

'Guv, whilst picking up Christopher Dolsen at the tattoo shop, we gained access to the upstairs flat.'

'And…'

'We found some coke.'

'How much?'

'Well, it looks like it had already been cut, or was in the process of being cut. We counted forty-two bags in total, but I reckon there might be about three kilos.'

'Excellent. Leave one of the uniformed officers on site and call in the forensic boys; your priority is to bring in Christopher Dolsen.'

'Understood, guv.'

Coker placed the phone back in his pocket. 'You hear that, Dolsen, we've just picked up three keys of coke at your tattoo studio.'

'It's not my tattoo studio.' Jimmy Dolsen thought about elaborating further, but consoled himself with the thought that, whilst inconvenient, the timing could not have been better, as tomorrow they were due to take a shipment of twenty kilos of coke and fifty-thousand ecstasy tablets, and the upstairs flat of the tattoo studio would have been the first location where the shipment was to be held. He allowed himself a little smile.

It would probably have been far easier to concentrate the eleven across one or two stations, but DI Coker was adamant that from the point of arrest, none of the Dolsen gang were to see or speak to each other. Five police stations had been selected, of a relatively large size, having a total of twenty-seven holding cells between them; thus even with a few already occupied, there was sufficient space to keep them all apart. Jimmy Dolsen was being taken to Manchester's Central Park station.

The unmarked police car drove through the barrier and into the secure area; the steel gates closed behind them and DI Coker assisted his handcuffed guest out of the rear seats. They walked through a door above which, screwed to the wall, was a simple sign that read *Custody Suite*. They went through a series of two secure doors, and finally into the suite. It didn't faze Jimmy Dolsen one bit; he had been arrested before, he had been through a

number of these custody areas over the years. DI Coker
led him to the desk.

'My name is Sergeant Joblin, and I'm the custody sergeant. Whilst you are in the custody suite, you are my
responsibility, and I am responsible for your health and
protection, and well as ensuring that the investigative process is progressing within the time limits we have in place.
Do you understand?'

No comment.

'I'll take that as a yes.'

No comment.

'Right, let's get you booked in. Name?'

'Dolsen, James Dolsen.'

Sergeant Joblin looked up from the keyboard and
smirked. 'Is that like Bond, James Bond?'

'No it's not, you fucking halfwit.'

That was the pleasantries done then. The next five
minutes was spent gathering and documenting Jimmy
Dolsen's personal details, advising him of his right to free
legal representation, and DI Coker conveying details of his
arrest. Jimmy was shipped off to the biometric room for
fingerprints, photographs and a DNA sample.

'What about my phone call?' asked Dolsen.

'Your phone call?' replied Coker, 'you've been watching
too many episodes of *Blue Bloods* on Sky.'

After an all too brief chuckle, the custody sergeant
chipped in, 'you are allowed to nominate someone who is
likely to have an interest in your welfare; someone that we
will contact on your behalf.'

Now Coker started to laugh. 'You've got no-one left,
Dolsen, we've rounded them all up. Everyone is in custody;
you, Davey, Christopher, a dozen or so of your lads. We've

even got some PC's bringing all the wives and girlfriends in as we speak. Fuck it, we might even go back and round up your children.' Jimmy made a lunge towards him but was held back by two uniformed custody officers. 'Having said that, we might just leave the kids at home for twenty-four hours, see how they fend for themselves. A social experiment. What do you think of that, Dolsen, James Dolsen?' said with a Sean Connery-esque Bond voice.

'Fuck off.'

'The fact is, Jimmy, detainees do not have a legal right to a phone call. This really isn't *Blue Bloods*,' he said as he gestured towards the open door of the cell some five metres behind, 'now, be a good boy and off you pop.'

Coker walked back to the main booking-in desk, and his mobile phone rang.

'Guv, it's Bowen.'

'And…'

'We've got him now.'

'Excellent, where did you find him?'

'At his mother's house.'

'Excellent, well done. Take him to your designated station and process him.'

'Yes, guv, we're on our way.'

All eleven targets had now been apprehended, arrested and were either safely tucked away in, or en-route to, a police station. Job done.

CHAPTER 21

Just twenty-four hours had passed, and whilst *the Dolsen Eleven* as they were being dubbed, for no reason other than it was an effortless name for the collective, were in custody, the team from SOCA and the CPS had been busy arranging the appearance of said collective at the magistrates' court.

In order to expedite the process, it had been decided that all eleven would appear in court at the same time; and at ten-thirty a.m. on the dot, they began to walk from the holding cells underneath the court house and up the stairs. Their brief and brisk walk ended as the final step led into the dock at Manchester Magistrates Court.

Suited and booted to a man, they stood in silence as the three magistrates entered by a side door and took their seats. Were it just one of the defendants, their time in court would have been unlikely to exceed ten minutes, but as charges needed to be read and pleas heard from all eleven, it would take considerably longer.

One by one, they would all enter a *not guilty* plea to the same charges: importation of a controlled drug, and supply of a controlled drug. Christopher Dolsen, by virtue of the forty-two bags of cocaine found in the flat above the tattoo shop upon his arrest, was also charged with possession with intent to supply. This seemed somewhat trivial considering the other two, more serious, charges, but the team knew that if Christopher was to escape their clutches on the supply charges, he would almost definitely get put away for five to seven years on the lesser charge, which there was no possibility of him weaselling out of. On this separate charge, Christopher also entered a *not guilty* plea.

'The charges,' advised the senior magistrate, 'are of sufficient seriousness, that we are unable to deal with them here,' this came as no surprise to anyone, 'so, you will all be committed to crown court for trial, at a date to be decided.'

'Thank you, sir.' The defence counsel rose to his feet. 'Now, on behalf of each of the eleven defendants, I would like to make an application for bail.'

The prosecuting counsel from the CPS let out an uncontrolled laugh, for which he immediately apologised to the presiding bench and his opposing counsel.

'My clients are all law-abiding citizens, taken from their homes in the early hours of the morning. There is no evidence whatsoever that any of my clients are involved in drug distribution; and I would urge the court to grant the application of bail in order that they may return home to their families, prior to waiting out the many months before the proposed commencement of crown court proceedings.'

'Thank you, Mr Davis,' noted the senior magistrate, as he looked up and over the rim of his tortoiseshell glasses, 'and I assume, Mr Greenhalgh, that the prosecution opposes this application?'

The prosecutor took to his feet. 'Yes, sir, in the strongest possible terms. In our...' He was cut short.

'Yes, yes. I don't think that we need to hear your arguments, we are in agreement that bail is denied, and that the defendants shall be remanded in custody pending their trial, at the as yet to be appointed date.'

'If I may, sir?' Mr Greenhalgh, the CPS prosecutor, took to his feet once again. 'In placing these defendants on remand, the CPS asks for a further item for your consideration.'

'Yes, go on.'

'We request that three separate remand centres are selected for James Dolsen, David Dolsen and Christopher Dolsen.'

'And the other eight?' enquired one of the other magistrates.

'We have no specific requests for the other defendants, ma'am.'

'Very unusual, but perhaps understandable. We will retire for ten minutes and come back with our decision.'

The court stood as the three magistrates rose to their feet. After instructing the clerk of the court that the defendants should remain in the dock, they exited through the side door.

Barely seven minutes had gone by when the court room was ushered back to life again.

The senior magistrate cleared his throat. 'We have considered your application, and subject to additional confirmations to be obtained over the next few hours, our decision is thus: James Dolsen shall be remanded in custody at HMP Lincoln, David Dolsen at HMP Liverpool, and Christopher Dolsen shall be remanded in custody at HMP Leeds. All other defendants are to be remanded to the nearest remand centre, as per normal procedure, at HMP Manchester.'

DI Coker, sitting in the gallery, allowed himself a smile. It wasn't concluded by any stretch of the imagination, but this was yet another important step achieved.

CHAPTER 22

eet me in The Alchemist at 13:00 was the text message from DI Coker, received by Priest, shortly followed by *I'll be one with the red carnation in my coat, carrying a copy of The Times.*

'Look what this dickhead's put in his text.' Priest passed his phone to DS Stephens. She smiled and returned it to him.

It had been six months since Priest had last met with Coker, although they had spoken on a fairly regular basis since. The Alchemist was the closest bar to the crown court where DI Coker and Sergeant Thomas had spent their morning.

Sentencing completed, we're on our way, Priest received the text just as Coker and Thomas came through the door. Priest caught their eye.

'Well, are we celebrating?' Coker gave an exuberant smile and headed to the bar. Whilst it could probably have been gleaned purely on the strength of Coker's smile, Priest didn't need to wait long for his answer as he saw Coker winding his way over to their table with a bottle of bubbly and four glasses.

'I guess that answers my question then. Or at least, I hope it answers my question, and we're not commiserating and getting pissed on expensive champagne?'

'Nope, we're definitely celebrating.' Coker popped the cork and filled the glasses. 'A toast, to the British judicial system, to some good old fashioned police work; and to getting the likes of Dolsen off our streets for many, many years.'

DI Coker had attended some, but not all, of the three-week trial. As a witness for the prosecution, he had been summoned to attend within the first week, primarily in support of PC Darby's written evidence. Evidence that was submitted and accepted by the judge, despite Darby's absence. Coker had fought for weeks with the CPS to get them to prosecute, as the general feeling was that Darby's participation in the murder of Jarel Powell had simply discredited him too much, and this had tainted any evidence that he had gathered, of any nature, during his time as an undercover police officer.

It had taken many heated conversations before the CPS had agreed to prosecute, and DI Coker had, by all accounts, pushed the boundaries of acceptable levels of dialogue with the CPS. In the end, their decision was seen as quite a coup for SOCA and police forces nationwide, as the CPS didn't often make decisions based on verbal pressure applied from police officers, irrespective of their seniority or the importance of the case at hand. The CPS, or course, were quick to point out that their U-turn was nothing to do with police pressure, and all to do with *a brave and visionary stance from the Chief Crown Prosecutor, Sandra McHale.*

Such was the importance of the trial to Coker, and across SOCA; he had the clerk of the court call him at the end of every day in order to provide a ten-minute update on the highs and lows of the day's proceedings. Such engagement wasn't strictly allowed, but the clerk was an ex-police officer, and had known Coker for a dozen years or more. He knew that the daily updates were important to Coker, and knew that it would be the only way to prevent him from attending court every day.

Coker was hoping to hold out for the big score, an opportunity to mount a successful sting operation that would have caught them red-handed, and in relation to the Dolsens, a situation of significant importance that would have seen Jimmy in attendance too. He was hoping for the kind of one-off operation that might see them nabbed for large-scale distribution, and relative jail terms of twenty-five years or more. Alas, the opportunity to mount an operation never came; and with no undercover officer in place, they needed to salvage something from the last two years, and this was probably the best that they could hope for.

Listen, I'll be happy if they get between five and eight years, Coker had been heard to say at the start of the trial.

'Well,' said Priest, 'what was the result?'

Coker beamed with a smile that simply radiated, and his grin was replicated by DS Thomas. 'Jimmy Dolsen received sixteen years, Davey Dolsen received fourteen years and Christopher Dolsen received fourteen years too.'

Priest was about to speak, but realised Coker hadn't finished. His pause was simply a brief reflection on the magnitude of their success.

'Three others, Lambert, Kiveton and Woolhouse, all received eight years each.'

'Excellent,' Priest declared, and raised his glass prompting another celebratory chinking, 'well done,' and yet Priest could see that Coker was dying to continue; he hadn't finished yet.

'Their assets have been seized too: houses, cars, night-clubs, pubs, a tattoo shop, plus five lock-up garages. It could be up to eight or nine million in value.'

'Bloody good result all round, I'd say,' confirmed Priest, 'well done.'

'Eighty-six, was it, sergeant?'

'It was, guv,' confirmed DS Thomas, 'eighty-six.'

'Eighty-six years imprisonment in total was handed down to eleven members of the Dolsen gang.'

'That's their entire empire well and truly dismantled now,' said Stephens, 'all the top dogs plus their immediate lieutenants; surely their whole infrastructure from import to local distribution must have crumbled now?'

'I agree,' said Coker, 'I can't see the Dolsens recovering from this, although you know as well as I do that in a business governed by supply and demand, the void that has recently been created will be filled by someone.' Nods of unity and mutual agreement were received.

'It has been six months since we took Jimmy Dolsen into custody, and I dare say that forty percent of the volume that they controlled has been picked up by other, rival organised gangs. I reckon in about another twelve to eighteen months, the volume of coke, hash and E's floating around will be back to what it was just before we lifted Dolsen. In the interim, as with the basic laws of supply and demand, the prices on the street have just rocketed.'

'Bloody hell, how do you continue to motivate yourselves?' asked Stephens.

'Well, the very fact that that some other scumbag needs taking off the streets is motivation alone, and to be honest it's not too different to your role in CID.'

'How so?'

'Well, when you put away a burglar or murderer, it doesn't prevent or wholly deter others from committing burglary or murder, does it?'

'No, I guess not.'

'No, you put one away behind bars, then another one comes along next week, next month, next year.'

'Or another four all at once,' Priest added. Stephens nodded her agreement, cognisant of their current case load.

'It's never ending; it will never end,' advised Coker, 'not in my time on the force anyway.'

'Yes, sadly too true.'

'So you keep going, and with God's grace, in twelve months' time, we'll have another scumbag drug dealer and gang leader off the streets for ten to twenty years.'

'I'm not so sure about God's grace having any tangible impact, but I know what you mean.'

After a refresh of their drinks, DI Coker continued to provide a precis of the last three weeks' court action, although his less than brief overview could easily have been a reading from the entire court transcript. 'The judge indicated to the jury to accept the written reports of PC Darby as authentic, as though he had appeared in court himself.'

'Well, that was positive,' noted Stephens, 'I guess it might have been a different outcome if PC Darby's reports, and Simon Darby himself, had been discredited completely.'

'Correct,' noted Coker, nothing if not succinct.

Jimmy Dolsen had apparently instructed his barrister to ensure that Darby's participation in the murder of Jarel Powell was made known in open court. Jimmy was looking to discredit Darby, and thus all of his evidence. His barrister had warned against this approach for fear that it would backfire, and it did, spectacularly.

The prosecuting barrister thought all of his birthdays had arrived at once, as the explanation of Darby's involvement in Powell's murder could only be explained by widening the dialogue to explore the whole feud between the Yardies and the Dolsens. This in turn led to too many uncomfortable questions on drug import, supply and distribution; the answers to which neither Jimmy nor Davey fared well under cross examination.

'The judge in his sentencing recognised this as somewhat of a landmark case, in that the heavy sentences were passed down even though none of the defendants had actually been caught in possession of any drugs; well, with the exception of Christopher and the stash we found when he was picked up.'

They all took a moment to ponder.

'So, tell me, how are you getting on with your own investigation, the murder enquiries?' asked Coker.

'We mopped up the Jarel Powell case about the same time as you picked up Jimmy Dolsen, and much of that was based on Darby's confession, so that one is closed. Victoria Dolsen was undoubtedly a revenge murder carried out by the Yardies, but the case remains open, as does that of Shaun Dolsen and PC Simon Darby. Arguably, her boyfriend was in the wrong place at the wrong time too, so his attempted murder remains open too. To be honest, we are unlikely to make much progress beyond this point; to be able to gather any credible evidence, we need an undercover officer in the Yardie gang.' Priest had said this somewhat tongue in cheek, although that was exactly what he needed at this point.

'Not likely to happen with any serving police officer, I wouldn't think; your best bet is to try and turn one of the existing gang members into an informant.'

'Yeah, although it'll be easier to get my white eighty-four-year-old grandma accepted into their ranks, I would have thought.' The comment drew howls of laughter from the quartet.

'On these three specific murders we might have to accept defeat, at least for now. You never know what might happen over the next few weeks, months, or years.'

Priest turned to Coker. 'We might not have the result that we wanted yet, but SOCA must be pleased with what you've achieved. Pat on the back and promotions all around, I would expect?'

'Ha, not sure about the promotions, but a well-deserved pat on the back for the team, that's for sure.'

Priest picked up his glass and held it aloft. 'Well here's to eighty-six years of peace and quiet on the streets of Manchester.'

A further, and final, chink of glasses followed, accompanied by a raucous outburst of laughter.

An hour later, after DI Coker and DS Thomas had left, DCI Priest and DS Stephens were on their own, doing their utmost to drink the house dry of red wine.

'I think you and I need a change of scenery, Nic,' noted Priest, 'do you fancy a spell in the Serious Organised Crime Agency?'

'No, you're alright, Jonny. Manchester CID is more than enough excitement for me.'

THE END